# "Why don't we discuss my duties?"

Sami shrugged. "Since my mother hired you, perhaps you should be asking her what she wants from you."

"I've already explained this," Noah replied. "I've been instructed to give you whatever you want."

"I want a baby." Had she really said that? It was the truth and for some reason she couldn't seem to help provoking him with it. "Were you offering your services in that department, too?"

His gaze never left her as he approached. "Do you want me to take you to bed, Sami?"

**Day Leclaire** and her family live in the midst of a maritime forest on a small island off the coast of North Carolina. Despite the yearly storms that batter them and the frequent power outages, they find the beautiful climate, superb fishing and unbeatable seascape more than adequate compensation. One of their first acquisitions upon moving to Hatteras Island was a cat named Fuzzy. He has recently discovered that laps are wonderful places to curl up and nap—and that Day's son really was kidding when he named the hamster Cat Food.

**Recent titles by the same author:**

SHOTGUN BRIDEGROOM
HER SECRET SANTA
BRIDEGROOM ON APPROVAL
LONG-LOST BRIDE

# HER SECRET BODYGUARD

BY

## DAY LECLAIRE

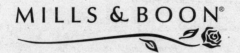

**MILLS & BOON®**

To Nancy. You're with us, still.

*First published in Great Britain 2000*
*Harlequin Mills & Boon Limited,*
*Eton House, 18-24 Paradise Road, Richmond, Surrey TW9 1SR*

© Day Totton Smith 2000

ISBN 0 263 82066 1

*Set in Times Roman 10½ on 12 pt.*
02-0004-46182

*Printed and bound in Spain*
*by Litografía Rosés, S.A., Barcelona*

# PROLOGUE

"WHAT do you mean I'm too old to have six children?" Sami Fontaine demanded. "I'm still in my twenties. I have plenty of time."

Rosie—Sami's sometime housekeeper and all-the-time best friend—had the unmitigated gall to snort. "Give it up, sweetie. I've known you for years now. Ever since you rescued me from that awful maid's job next door. You're the same age I am. That means you've left the big three-oh behind and are rapidly sliding into a solid over-the-hill thirty-one."

Sami scowled. "Not until next week."

Rosie leaned back against the couch cushions and rested her teacup and saucer on top of her heavily pregnant belly. "Be reasonable." She ticked off on her fingers. "You don't have a husband. You don't even have a boyfriend. Assuming you find the love of your life within the next year and marry, you'll be pushing thirty-two before you have your first kid."

"So?"

"Do the math. Are you planning on having a baby a year?"

Sami's jaw inched out. "Maybe."

Rosie gave another of her annoying little snorts. "Not a chance. You know full well it's not healthy for you or your children. Look at my relatives. Carmela and Daria have six children between them and they barely have a brain cell to rub together. Those kids run them ragged.

You watch." She patted her belly. "As soon as I have junior, here, I won't have a brain, either."

"But they're such sweet kids," Sami said wistfully.

"I adore them to pieces, too. But it takes four adult women to keep six kids in line. What does that tell you?"

Sami shot her friend a mischievous grin. "That we're rotten disciplinarians?"

"You're getting off track."

"I excel at that."

"We've all noticed." Rosie took a quick sip of tea, her expression growing serious. "Let's figure this out logically."

"Let's not. You know how I hate logical people." Sami made a face. "They're so...*logical*."

"You mean sensible."

"Even worse," Sami said with a shudder.

"Honey, if you're going to have a baby, you don't have much choice. You have to be sensible."

Sami released her breath in a gusty sigh. "All right, hit me. How am I not being sensible?"

"If you space your pregnancies two years apart, you're talking about twelve years. That's pushing it age-wise, Sami. Do the math," she instructed again.

"I've never been particularly good at calculations."

"No, you've never been particularly good at facing facts. Why, you'd be popping out that sixth one when you're in your forties! Do you realize how old that'll make you when your youngest graduates from high school? Assuming you survive that long with your sanity intact. *And* assuming all your parts haven't already at-rophied."

"Atrophied!"

Rosie swept her hand through the air, the teacup rattling in its saucer. "Hey, you snooze, you lose. When's the last time you gave everything a good shakedown? Run your engine at full throttle?"

"I've throttled plenty," Sami insisted. "In fact, I'm thinking about throttling you right this very minute."

"That's not what I mean and you know it. You're afraid of marriage. Admit it."

"Fine. I'll admit it. I'm petrified of marriage."

"And we both know why." Rosie threw her a sympathetic look. "But it's a little tough to have kids without a father. Ask Daria. So unless you find a way past your aversion, I suggest you reconsider having babies anytime soon."

Sami drummed her fingers on the arm of her chair. "I hate being told no."

"Don't we all."

"I suppose. But you've always taken it a lot better than I have. So if marriage isn't a likely possibility and I really want a baby—" Sami broke off and chuckled. "I've got an idea. Good grief, I don't know why it didn't occur to me sooner."

"Sami—"

She rubbed her hands together. "It's perfect. Well, maybe perfect is a slight exaggeration. But it's close to perfect."

Rosie closed her eyes and groaned. "I don't even want to know. Just tell me I won't have to clean up after this brilliant idea of yours."

"No, you won't." Sami smiled expansively. "I'm sure Carmela and Daria will pitch in until after the baby's born."

"Whose?" Rosie retorted. "Yours or mine?"

"Don't be ridiculous. I mean yours. Mine is only in the planning stages."

"You're scaring me, Sami."

"You know what? I think I'm scaring myself." She grinned. "Isn't it great? I'm feeling so good about this idea I might even break down and make a list."

"A list?" Rosie snatched up Sami's teacup and sniffed it.

"What are you doing?"

"Checking for hallucinogens." Rosie shook her head and sighed. "It's clean. That can only mean one thing."

"What?"

"You've lost your mind."

"Have you lost your mind?"

Babe Fontaine threw herself into a black-and-white-striped chair and kicked off her shoes. "Now, sweetie," she said, fumbling for a pack of cigarettes. "That's not a very nice thing to say."

"You're right. It isn't." Noah Hawke crossed Babe Fontaine's carefully decorated Nob Hill living room in an effort to escape the smoke, his dog, Loner, followed at his heels. He halted in front of a huge picture window and allowed his gaze to drift from the gorgeous view of San Francisco sprawled below him to the sunlit bay glistening in the distance. "I apologize. I know it's not much of an excuse, but I just came off a tough project."

She threw him a sympathetic look. But then, that was Babe. "Were you able to help your client?"

"I'm always able to help my client. It's what I do best." He turned his back on the window. "Unfortunately, it didn't end well. I discovered her accountant was robbing her blind."

"Oh, Noah. That's awful. I hope you sicced your wolf on him."

"Wolves are wild animals," he explained gently. "It's illegal to own them. Since I own Loner, he can't be a wolf."

"Oh, pooh. You can't fool me, sweetie." She jumped to her feet and began pacing. Babe had never been one to sit still for long. She was a tiny dynamo of a woman with enough energy for half a dozen people. "I know a wolf when I see one." She stabbed her cigarette in Loner's direction. "And that guy over there has 'big' and 'bad'—not to mention, 'wolf'—written all over him."

"Since you're not Little Red Riding Hood, I don't think you need to worry."

Her explosive laughter filled the apartment. He'd always liked that about her, maybe because she was so different from him. Hell, he liked just about everything about Babe, despite her predilection for cigarettes. She was drop-dead gorgeous, with natural blond hair and vivid blue eyes, and she was also as open and direct as they came. He'd never known anyone quite so outgoing or down-to-the-bones nice. All in all, an intriguing package. Unfortunately, she also wanted something. And ten times out of ten, what Babe wanted, Babe got.

"I have work to do," he prompted. "Tell me why you really called."

"I already did." She drew on her cigarette and fixed him with a frank look. "You owe me, sweetie, and as much as I hate doing it, I'm calling in the debt."

"Let me get this straight. You're asking me to drop everything and play nanny to your daughter?" He couldn't believe it. "You're joking, right?"

"I've never been more serious in my life." To his concern, lines of strain etched a path across her porcelain complexion. "Noah, I need you, honey. I mean *really* need you. And you owe me."

That was a matter of opinion. As far he was concerned, he'd paid his debt and then some. Unfortunately, she didn't seem to realize that. "I have other commitments, Babe. I can't just drop everything and dedicate myself to... What's her name?"

"Sami."

Sami. He tried out the name, wondering if she'd be like Babe or the exact opposite. Somehow he couldn't believe there were two Babes in the world. All that wild energy running loose could be dangerous. "What sort of trouble is she in? What's she done?"

"She hasn't done a thing. It's what someone wants to do to her that's the problem."

He sighed. "Can the melodrama, Babe, and tell me the problem."

She immediately crossed to a small end table by the couch and yanked open the drawer. Removing a creamy white envelope, she handed it to him. "Read it."

He weighed it in his palm, running his fingers over the rich texture. "Nice quality."

"The best. Trust me, I know."

He could just make out the word *"Sami"* written on the outside in neat, precise handwriting. He slipped the single sheet of paper from the unsealed envelope and stared at the jumble of blurred words. With an impatient grimace, he reached in his pocket and withdrew a pair of reading glasses. He'd have thought after thirty-some years, he'd remember to wear the damn things. He scanned the note, then read it again, swearing beneath his breath. *"The time has come. Pay up or face the consequences."*

"Where did you find this?" he asked, returning the glasses to his pocket.

"I moved out of the house a few days ago to take up residence here, in the apartment. I found that note at the house."

"Getting married again?"

She chuckled, though there was an edge beneath the humor. "You sound like Sami. No, I didn't move out because I was planning to get married again, I just felt like a change of scenery. Anyway, when I stopped by the house to collect my mail, that envelope was mixed in with my stuff. I don't think Sami's even seen it. In fact, I'm sure she hasn't. She's not very good at keeping secrets."

"Have you called the police?"

*"No!"* She hastened to lower her voice. "No. I'd rather not do that. You're the hot-shot troubleshooter, so I called you." Apprehension dimmed the vividness of her eyes. "Please, don't involve the police. You have to promise me that."

"Why the hell not?"

"Because of the adverse publicity." She wrapped her arms around her waist. "I've got a funny feeling about this, Noah. I think it's someone Sami and I know."

"Since it wasn't sent through the mail, I'd say that's a reasonable assumption. Where did you find it?"

"On the table in the front hallway of the house." She ground out her cigarette in a gold-leaf ashtray. "If it *is* a friend or acquaintance, I'll want it handled quietly."

"Why?"

"Simple." A sad smile slipped across her face. "I like all the people I know."

"Aw, hell." Beside him, Loner whined.

Babe turned her gaze on the dog and nodded. "Yeah. My thoughts exactly, fella. Well?" Her attention switched back to Noah. "Will you do it?"

As far as he could see, he didn't have a choice. "What's your plan?"

"I want you to move in with her for a while. See what you can uncover."

"Are you going to warn her about the note?"

"No. And that's the other promise you'll have to make. You're not to tell her anything about this. Knowing my little girl she'll try to find the blackmailer on her own. Or she'll use herself as bait." Babe shrugged. "Who can say with Sami?"

"Like mother like daughter?"

She gave him an abashed look. "Something like that."

Great. Just great. "So I'm not to inform the police or tell Sami what I'm doing in her home. And my excuse for being there is…?"

"Simple." Babe shot him a sassy grin. "You're gonna be my little girl's birthday present."

# CHAPTER ONE

NOAH walked into Sami Fontaine's residence and straight into sheer chaos.

Men of every size, shape, and description were scattered throughout the foyer. Some were seated in a row of chairs lining the entranceway, others lounged on the wide sweeping stairway leading to the second story. And a few were even sprawled on the heartwood flooring.

Well, hell. What was this about? Noah signaled Loner to take a seat by the door while he analyzed the situation. Babe had decided that Sami needed a man around the house to help take care of the place—at least, that was the excuse they'd hatched to explain his presence. It would seem that Sami had come to the same conclusion and interviews were in progress.

Noah frowned. Open interviews were dangerous. Anyone could wander in posing as a prospective employee. He couldn't even tell who was in charge, which suggested that proper precautions weren't being taken. He scanned those in the foyer. Even as he did so, he realized the sheer futility of looking for Sami's blackmailer in a hallway full of strangers.

It could be any one of them…or none.

Damn it all! This wasn't his area of expertise. What if something went wrong? What if he screwed up? If he were smart, he'd make tracks for the nearest police station and dump the problem in their lap. No doubt Babe would end up in tears and Sami would learn the truth, but at least he'd have acted responsibly. Before he could put thought into action, a tall, slender man erupted from a room off to one side of the foyer.

"Lady, you're nuts!" he announced.

A woman appeared in the doorway behind him. "My ad was quite clear, Mr. Griffith. It's not my fault that you're not perfect for the job."

Sami, Noah decided. It had to be. She hovered at the threshold, an outpouring of sunshine from the room they'd vacated exploding around her, embracing the untamed golden curls that haloed a sweet, mischievous face. She wasn't much taller than Babe, though her curves were a bit more generous. Nor was she as classically beautiful. Her face tended toward a triangular shape rather than oval, with high, slanted cheekbones, large pale eyes framed by a sweep of thick lashes, and a chin that warned of a stubborn nature.

But she radiated the same fierce intensity as Babe, as if her life essence had been packed in a vessel too small to contain it. Barefoot and with a face clean of makeup, she wore blazing orange Capri slacks, the calf length showing off slender ankles and hugging womanly hips. She'd topped the slacks with an eye-watering lime green cropped shirt that gave him a tantalizing glimpse of her flat stomach and trim waist. From head to toe, everything about her expressed a delicious vivaciousness.

She shook a scrap of newspaper at Griffith, a half dozen rainbow-hued bracelets jangling on her wrist. "It's all right here." She stepped into the foyer, stalking the unfortunate Griffith. "What part of my advertisement didn't you understand?"

"The part about you being crazy!" He whirled around to address the others in the hallway. "If you were smart you'd get out while you have the chance. Run, before it's too late!''

Noah assessed his options and reached a swift decision. If he were going to fulfill his obligation to Babe, he couldn't afford to let anyone else accept the position Sami was advertising. Despite Griffith's failure, the hallway overflowed with potential successes—something he'd have to deal with and fast. He gave Loner a quick hand signal, then with a practiced economy of movement, accessed the room Sami had vacated, his dog at his heels. He doubted anyone noticed. Not while a woman like Sami held center stage.

''Mr. Griffith! You're not acceptable for the position, but that doesn't mean one of these other gentlemen won't be perfect. Please don't attempt to drive off other prospective applicants just because you have a nasty case of sour grapes.'' She waved toward the front door, her bracelets spinning around her wrist so fast the colors blurred. ''I suggest you leave.''

''Fine, I'm going.'' He marched in the direction she indicated and paused. ''As for the rest of you... Don't say you weren't warned. She has some pretty peculiar ideas about the man she considers perfect for this job.''

The instant he left, Sami kicked the door closed so hard, the leaded-glass windows fronting the house rattled in their frames. Noah shook his head in wry amusement. It was a wonder she didn't bruise her toes—toes, he couldn't help noticing, accented with hot pink nail polish. Where did she come up with her color combinations, anyway? Maybe she closed her eyes and picked whatever hideous shade came to hand.

Shoving curls from her eyes, she turned to confront the rest of the men in the hallway, her frown blossoming into a wide, teasing grin. Noah froze. He wasn't often taken by surprise. In fact, he took pains to ensure such an uncomfortable event happened as infrequently as possible. But that one smile astonished the hell out of him. It also transformed Sami into something beyond beauty.

The chatter died as all eyes focused on her in utter fascination. Impressive, Noah decided. Without saying a word, she commanded everyone's attention. Her personality was that magnetic. She'd become a flamboyant siren, a female Pied Piper who led willing men to their doom. Hell. It would take a unique man to resist the promise of that smile. Which meant he'd better figure out how to become "unique" or he'd find himself up to his hips in disaster.

"Okay, you've been warned," she announced with a quicksilver laugh. Did she even realize the reaction her laugh stirred in the men grouped around her? Somehow, he didn't think so. "So who's my next victim?"

A momentary silence reigned and Noah cleared his throat. "Ready, willing and able."

She spun around and blinked in surprise. "Oh, I didn't see you there. Are you the next applicant?"

With the light behind him, Noah doubted she could get a clear look at his face. But he could see hers. Up close, he found her even more appealing. He particularly liked her eyes. They had to be the palest green he'd ever seen, the irises ringed with a darker shade. He'd never met anyone with such an open, candid expression. This was not a woman accustomed to keeping secrets from the world.

He sighed. In other words…trouble.

"Hey! That's not right," one of the men in the hallway protested. "I was next in line."

Not anymore, Noah decided. Sami was about to interview her last job applicant. "Loner, guard."

The dog trotted from the room and planted himself in the middle of the hallway, baring an impressive set of teeth. A rumbling growl reverberated deep in his throat.

The man held up his hands and backed away. "My mistake. I meant I was next after you."

Nodding in satisfaction, Noah gave Loner another hand signal and grasped Sami's arm, ushering her neatly over the threshold and into the parlor. Then he swung the door closed, closeting them in the room together.

"That was impressive," she said. "Were you really next?"

"No."

"So you're cutting in line." Her mouth twitched. "Don't you think that's a little unfair to the other applicants?"

"Not even a little. I want the job more than they do."

"Seriously?"

"I wouldn't joke about something that important."

"You know…" She glanced at the closed door and frowned. "Your dog looks like a wolf."

He took the change of subject in stride, half expecting it, given her relationship to Babe. "There's a slight resemblance."

"More than slight." She crossed to the desk occupying one end of the room and delved into a gold foil box of chocolates that stood open next to a stuffed animal. Ironically, it was a wolf cub. A bit battered, but recognizable nonetheless. She tickled it with the tip of her index finger. "In my opinion, he looks a lot like a wolf."

She was persistent, he'd give her that. Not many people pushed for more information than he willingly offered. For some reason they found him intimidating, something he did little to discourage. Perhaps it was because he favored black, a color that suited his solitary nature. Or perhaps his expression deterred familiarity. How many times had he been told that his silver-gray eyes were unsettling or that his quietness unnerved people or that his dispassion built insurmountable walls? A rare smile relaxed his mouth. Or perhaps it wasn't him at all, but Loner who scared them spitless.

Sami tilted her head to one side, wayward curls caressing a long, pale neck. "Aren't you going to answer me?"

"Okay. Loner looks a lot like a wolf."

"Loner?" She returned the stuffed wolf cub to the desk and approached. "That's an interesting name."

"It suits him."

"I'd say it suits his master, as well."

She'd roused his curiosity. "What makes you think that?"

"I'm good at reading people. And you—" To his utter astonishment, she thumped his chest with her index finger. She was either a brave woman or a foolish one, he couldn't quite decide which. "—you're very self-contained. Self-sufficient. A man who walks his own path. Am I right or am I right? You're a loner, too."

He shrugged. "I've been called worse."

"So is he one?" As though anticipating his confusion over the question, she graced him with another of her high-voltage smiles. "Is Loner a wolf, I mean."

"That would be illegal," he explained gently. "It's against the law for private individuals to own or house wild animals."

"And you wouldn't do anything illegal?"

He could see lying to her was going to be a problem. Something about those clear green eyes—eyes that saw straight through to his soul—had the power to force the truth from him. Yeah. This lady was trouble incorporated. Perhaps misdirection would work. He folded his arms across his chest. "How about starting the interview?"

"We already have."

Uh-oh. "Talking about Loner is part of the interview process?"

She inclined her head. "Discussing your honesty is."

"You want the truth?"

"I always want the truth."

Right. How many times had he heard that from a woman? Then he'd oblige, the tears would start and he'd end up wishing he'd said something on the shady side of honest, if only so it would be a bit less hurtful. "I found Loner abandoned as a pup. He'd been injured. You may have noticed he still walks with a limp?"

"Poor thing," she murmured, genuinely sympathetic.

"I suspect he's part wolf, though when I eventually tracked down the owner, we never got around to the subject."

That snagged her attention. "You tracked down the owner?"

"Yes."

"The one who'd abandoned Loner."

"Right."

"Whatever for?"

Noah released his breath in a long sigh. He couldn't remember the last time he'd had to explain himself to someone. He also couldn't remember the last time he'd wanted to. But with Sami… "I needed to explain to him the importance of taking proper care of his animals."

Comprehension dawned. "I see. And did he survive your…er…explanation?"

"Let's say he won't be making the same mistake again."

"Good." She fixed him with a direct look that combined approval with admiration. It shouldn't please him, but it did. "I assume Loner's been with you ever since?"

"Anywhere I go, he goes." Perhaps he should make himself a little clearer on that point. "Without exception."

She lifted an eyebrow. "Even to bed?" she asked irrepressibly.

"In the bedroom, at the foot of the bed."

"But not in it?"

"You ask some mighty peculiar questions, lady." Her gaze remained trained on him and he sighed. "No. Not in it."

"I thought we should clarify that up front."

"Why?"

"Because it's my bed you'll be sleeping in."

"So the position comes with room and board?"

"The position?" She chuckled. "Cute. Look, why don't we sit down and get to know each other a little better, Mr—?" She stopped short. "Good grief. I can't believe we've been talking all this time and haven't introduced ourselves."

"It's Noah."

She held out her hand, bracelets jangling. "I'm Sami Fontaine. So is Noah your first name or your last?"

This was where matters got sticky. The next few

minutes would be crucial. If she didn't accept what he told her, he'd soon follow the hapless Mr. Griffith out the front door, the rich golden oak kissing his backside. "First."

"And your last?"

"Hawke."

She stilled. "Hawke?" Her brow wrinkled. "Hawke. Hawke. I know that name. But from where?"

He turned his back on her and crossed to a cluster of chairs where she'd been conducting her interviews. Papers were strewn across the table in the middle of the sitting area. He didn't wait for an invitation, but took a seat. "So what questions do you have for me?"

She snapped her fingers. "I've got it. My mother once planned to marry a man with that last name." She followed him to the sitting area. "Mel Hawke. Have you heard of him? Are you related?"

"I believe there's a connection," he admitted casually. "In fact, that's how I came to hear about the job."

"Excuse me?" Sami sank into the chair opposite of his, her eyes so wide they threatened to engulf her face. "Mel told you about my ad? He *knows?* How in the world would he—"

"Actually, it was your mother who suggested I come here."

"My *mother!*" Her breathing quickened, her cropped shirt doing an intriguing dance just above her belly button. "I can't believe it. My mother suggested— How? Why? When?"

He fell silent and waited. It was an effective technique. It took a bit longer than average for Sami to catch on, but the instant she did, her agitation faded. Curling her legs onto the chair beneath her, she cupped her chin in her palm, her eyes glittering with good-natured humor.

"You're waiting for me to be quiet so you can answer all my questions, aren't you?"

"If you don't mind."

"I do have a tendency to interrupt." She released her breath in a gusty sigh and shoved curls from her face. They shivered around her head with a life of their own, sparkling with gold fire. Fascinating. "I guess this is a good time to confess that whenever something occurs to me, I just open my mouth and say what's on my mind. I put it right out there."

"No filters or limits?" He didn't know why he bothered phrasing that as a question. He already knew the answer.

"None."

"That must make for an interesting life."

"Very." She leaned forward and lowered her voice. "When I was little, I'd get into trouble for it all the time. I swear I spent more hours in the principal's office than in the classroom. That probably doesn't come as much surprise to you though, huh? I never did outgrow the habit, but now I'm old enough that people consider me eccentric rather than troublesome." She paused briefly. "So. You were going to tell me about my mother."

"Was I?"

"Absolutely."

For someone who liked drifting off on tangents, she had an uncanny knack of returning to the original path. Too bad. He'd have been happier ducking this particular question. "I'm your birthday present," he offered up Babe's outrageous lie.

To his surprise Sami sat for a full minute, her lush

mouth gaping. A hint of color inched along her angled cheekbones. "Are you serious? My mother really knows what I'm doing? And she…" Sami fought for breath, on the verge of hyperventilating. "She *sent* you? For my *birthday?* She *approves?*"

Somehow he'd managed to step on a land mine. No doubt he'd find it a regular occurrence around Sami. "Why so surprised?" he asked cautiously. "You're all grown up and perfectly capable of conducting your life as you see fit, aren't you?"

Sami cleared her throat. "Well, yes. But my mother tends to be a bit conservative, despite her various engagements and marriages. Maybe because of them."

He struggled to decipher what she meant by that. "So you don't think Babe will approve of your having a man here when you're not married?" How odd. He wouldn't have thought someone as self-assured as Sami would get uptight over her mother's opinion. It also didn't make sense considering that every last prospective employee decorating her front hallway was male.

"It's not that—"

"I think Babe can assure you I'm safe to have around."

"I don't doubt that. But… You're certain about this?" Sami probed. "She doesn't object?"

"Positive. Babe explained that the job might be temporary, so she's willing to pay for the first three months of service. After that, we can renegotiate."

To his surprise, her blush intensified. It mystified him. In the hallway she'd taken charge without hesitation. Was it all an act, camouflage to hide a more sensitive disposition? It disappointed him. He'd been drawn to her outrageousness, perhaps because it was the exact opposite of his own. Still, he preferred the truth above all else, despite the lie he had to currently enact. He frowned. Perhaps it would be best if he tried to ease her concerns.

"Does it matter that Babe recommended me for the job?" he asked. "Think of it as a family affair."

He'd chosen the wrong thing to say. She choked. "Let's not."

"Considering I came at Babe's request, can you at least agree to use my services instead of wasting time with more interviews?"

She shook her head. "I don't consider these interviews a waste of time. This is a serious decision, one I don't take lightly."

Smart woman. "Then let's continue with the interview until you're ready to reach a decision. I gather you have more questions."

"Lots of questions," she instantly replied.

"Go ahead. Hit me. I'd like to get this settled."

For some odd reason it took her a minute to gather herself. *Why?* The question nagged at him. He had the unsettling impression that something wasn't quite right and he'd learned long ago to listen to his instincts, though he'd have sooner cut out his tongue than admit that's what they were. Instead, he called them logical deductions based on a subconscious awareness of facts not immediately in evidence. And sitting here, listening to her, he was profoundly aware that there was a slew of facts not immediately in evidence. Sami's reaction to their interview struck him as too extreme.

Oh, yeah. She was trouble, no doubt about it.

"How old are you?" she finally asked.

"Thirty-five."

"Are you married?"

"No."

"Do you have any children?"

"No."

"What do you do for a living?"

Aw, hell. He hadn't expected that question. If he was here to work as her man Friday, what he did for a living should be self-evident. "Do you mean before this?"

"Mr. Hawke—"

"Noah."

"Noah, then. It's not like this is a full-time position."

"It's not?"

"After…after your—" She waved a hand in the air. "—*duties* are through for the day, you're free to go about your business. In fact, I don't expect you to spend much of your day here at all. If you wish to seek employment in addition to this, that's perfectly acceptable."

That wouldn't do. If he had a hope in hell of finding out who'd sent Sami that note, he'd have to be with her as close to twenty-four hours a day as possible. Maybe he'd give her a little nudge in the appropriate direction. "I was instructed to be at your disposal at all times. Since I'm being paid—and paid well—to take care of your needs, that's what I intend to do. Tell me how, when and where, and I'm on top of it."

"How?" she repeated faintly. "You need to know… *how?*"

What the *hell* was her problem? He regarded her with ill-disguised impatience. "You'll give me instructions, right? Or do you expect me to guess the way you want things done?"

"Oh, dear heaven." She buried her face in her hands.

"I can't believe this. I should have gone to the clinic. It would have been easier. But did I? Oh, no. I just had to do this my way. I had to take care of matters personally."

Clinic? Did they have clinics for hiring employees? It was a new one on him. Perhaps she meant an employment agency. And why was she overreacting to everything he said? It seemed so out of character for someone like Sami. He was fairly accurate at summing up people, an occupational hazard, he supposed. From the start, she'd struck him as capable, extroverted and even aggressive. So why did she find the process of hiring a man for general household duties so difficult? Hadn't she done this before? She acted as though she'd find giving orders an impossible task.

Enough was enough. "Is something wrong?" he asked.

"I just didn't expect…" She peeked at him from between her fingers. "You said you were thirty-five. Don't you know what to do?"

"Sure, in general. But I prefer specific instructions on the way *you* want things done. Most people have particular requirements. I'll need some idea of how to best accommodate your preferences."

That seemed to relieve her a bit. Her hands dropped to her lap, though her cheeks remained on the rosy side. "I hadn't thought of that."

"Look… Babe has already arranged this as your birthday present. Why don't you give me a trial run? We can set a time limit of say a month or six weeks. If I don't perform to expectations, we'll call it quits. If you're happy with the arrangement, we'll keep going the full three months she's paid for. Satisfaction guaranteed. How does that sound?''

''Perform to expectations?'' she repeated, appearing a bit stunned.

Okay. Maybe she was on the slow side. Flamboyant, but slow. Maybe Babe had a serious case of butterfingers and as an infant Sami's little head had been dribbled like a basketball. He should be gentle. Kind. Understanding. ''If you like what I do, you can keep me,'' he said, sticking to a single-syllable explanation.

It didn't seem to help. Her eyes darkened a shade. ''No way. Once you've…you've—how did you put it? Oh, right. Once you've performed to expectation and guaranteed my satisfaction, you're out of here. Got that?''

No. Not even a little. Not that he had the chance to say as much.

''Wait a minute! I understand now.'' She exploded from the chair, pacing in front of him. She ticked off on her fingers. ''You're a man. You're single. You're thirty-five. And you're suggesting this might turn into a long-term commitment. Babe wants you to marry me, doesn't she?''

''What the *hell* are you—''

She cut him off with a sweep of her hand. ''Don't bother denying it. My mother has been trying to marry me off for the past decade.'' As though aware she'd given out too much information, she added, ''For the past decade since I was *under* twenty, that is. Well under.''

''I am *not* interested in marriage.''

Sami dismissed his comment with an indelicate snort.

"It doesn't matter what either of us is interested in. It's Babe. She's trying her hand at matchmaking. Again."

Noah stood and grasped Sami's shoulders, planting her back into the chair she'd vacated. "No," he stated in his most forcible tone. "She is not."

"Ha! You don't know, Babe."

"Yes, I do know Babe." To his relief, that managed to shut her up. "Now pay attention, sweetheart. For your information, I'm not here to marry you. I'm here in response to your ad. That's it. I'm a birthday present, not a potential husband. Are we clear on that point?"

"Then why do you want to stay longer than three months?" she asked, suspicion clear in her voice.

"I didn't know how long you'd need me. Satisfaction guaranteed, remember?"

"Oh." She took a minute to ponder that. "You're sure Babe isn't trying to marry us off?"

"Positive." At least, he hoped not. That angle hadn't occurred to him before. Now that Sami had mentioned it, though, he'd be on his guard.

"I'm holding you to that promise," she warned.

A second possibility occurred, a far more probable one. Sami was a nutcase. Now that he thought about it, it seemed like more than a possibility and closer to a fact of nature. It would also explain why someone had decided to blackmail her. He could only guess what sort of trouble she'd stirred up to prompt such a threat. Time to move the interview along. The sooner he took on this job, the sooner it would end.

"Once you hire me, you can hold me to whatever promises you want. I don't mind."

She studied him for a moment, before nodding in satisfaction. "Okay, fine. Next issue. If I decide to accept your application, you'll need to have a physical exam."

What the hell for? He restrained himself from asking quite that bluntly. If her stubborn chin was any indication, she'd balk if he pushed too hard. He attempted to soft-pedal his demand. "Mind telling me why I need a physical?"

"I'd think that was obvious."

Aw, hell. "Maybe we should agree right now not to assume what should be obvious to the other. I've found it's usually best to spell things out so there aren't any misunderstandings."

"That sounds reasonable."

She'd recovered her equilibrium, though she still struck him as being about as far from an employer as anyone could possibly get. It was a good thing he'd arrived when he had or she'd have hired the first person shrewd enough to realize she was a few cans short of a six-pack and bulldoze over any and all objections.

"I need you to have an exam to make sure there aren't any physical defects that would prevent you from fulfilling your part of our agreement. In this day and age it's only sensible to be cautious."

He fought down a sense of outrage. "Are you afraid I'm going to give you some sort of disease?"

She stilled, a rarity for her, he'd bet. Even her bracelets fell silent. She studied him intently, as though attempting to gauge his emotional state. "Did my mother already have you examined?" she asked cautiously.

"No! Why would she do that?"

She folded her arms across her chest. "In that case, I'm afraid I'll have to insist. I'll also have to insist on complete references and a résumé. Then there's the contract.''

''Contract?''

''You realize you'll have to relinquish all responsibility and control once our—'' Her hand flitted through the air again, her bracelets repeating their enthusiastic jangling. ''—our association ends? When you leave here, I'll expect you to stay out of my life forever.''

''Don't you consider that a bit extreme?''

''Not even a little,'' she retorted defensively. ''Look… I could have gone to a clinic, you know.''

She'd mentioned that before. This time he decided to follow up on it. ''A clinic? Don't you mean a referral service or agency?''

''No, I mean a clinic. If I'd been smart, I'd have had the procedure done there. That way I'd never have known the donor and he'd never have known me. It would have been handled anonymously and I wouldn't have to worry about any future contacts between us.''

''A donor.'' Maybe he was the slow one. Maybe his six-pack had come up a few cans shy. Or maybe he needed to drink a few of those cans in order to understand just what the devil she was talking about. ''You did say a donor, correct?''

A frown lined her brow and she gazed at him in concern. ''Why do you keep repeating everything? Are you… Are you all right?''

She put enough emphasis on her final two words to royally tick him off. She was the crazy one, not him. And if she didn't know it, he'd be only too pleased to explain it to her. ''Do you remember when I asked that we spell everything out and not assume we knew what the other person meant?'' he asked.

"Yes."

"Well, I need you to start doing that." He stopped her before she could escape from her chair. "Before you go flitting around the room again, I want you to explain something to me."

She released an exasperated sigh. "What do you need explained?"

"I'm going to ask you a question and you're to be as clear and concise in your response as possible. Got that?"

"Clear and concise. Got it."

"Okay. Now. What donor are you talking about and what clinic?"

"A sperm donor at a fertility clinic." She stared in bewilderment. "What do you think we've been talking about all this time?"

# CHAPTER TWO

NOAH stared in utter disbelief. "You're hiring someone to *what?*"

Sami erupted from her chair. Why did he look so shocked? He said he'd been hired by her mother, that Babe knew about the ad. So why the sudden outrage? "To father my baby, of course. Isn't that what we've been discussing all this time?"

"It may have been what you were discussing, but—"

She attempted to walk off some of her agitation, the chatter of her bracelets drowning out his words. "Don't you understand? I chose this method because a clinic is so…so *clinical.* It's impersonal. I think that's terrible! Having a baby shouldn't be a clinical process. And it shouldn't be impersonal." She helped herself to another square of chocolate, savoring the creamy texture as it melted on her tongue. She instantly felt calmer. She held out the box. "Would you like one?"

"No. What I'd like is an explanation."

"You don't know what you're missing." Clearly the man had no appreciation for the finer epicurean treats in life. "I want to know all about the man who will father my son or daughter. I want to know what sort of genes will be combining with mine. What he looks like, what he thinks about, whether he has more than two brain cells rattling around in his skull."

"Whoa! Time out." He added something beneath his

breath, a ferocious slew of words she was better off not attempting to decipher.

She planted her hands on her hips and swiveled to face him. "What's wrong?"

"Is that what all those men in the hallway are for?"

"Of course."

"You're looking for someone to father your *baby?*"

Her frown deepened. "Maybe I should also schedule a psychological exam, just to play it safe."

"I suggest you schedule one for yourself, as well."

He climbed to his feet, towering over her. Maybe it was his penchant for wearing black she found intimidating. Really, couldn't he have softened the effect with a bit of lemony-yellow or peachy-coral? Or perhaps it wasn't the intense black at all, but the way his shirt stretched over impressively broad shoulders and clung to powerful thighs. Or maybe it was the manner in which he fixed those piercing gray eyes on her. It took every ounce of self-possession not to squirm like a schoolgirl. She hadn't felt this way since... Since... Well, good grief. Come to think of it, she'd *never* felt this way.

"Have you lost your mind?" he demanded.

As far as she was concerned, there was no question about it. She scowled. "I suspect I have. Maybe if you moved all—" She gestured at the muscular wall of black blocking her path. "All *that* further away, I could think straight."

His eyebrow—his *black* eyebrow—shot upward. Amusement dimmed the anger glittering in his gaze. "Am I standing too close?" he asked blandly.

"Yes. To be honest, I'm typically one of those people with little to no sense of personal space. But with you…'' She shook her head. ''I may have to install a buffer zone.''

He took a deliberate step backward. ''Better?''

''Much thanks.''

''Good. Now perhaps you can answer my questions. You put an ad in the newspaper for sperm donors?''

''Yes. Though I worded it a bit more politely than that.''

''How politely?''

She swept to the coffee table by the chairs, bracelets jangling in agitation, and picked up a scrap of newspaper. ''Didn't Babe show this to you?''

He took the ad from her and removed his reading glasses from his shirt pocket. Another frown lined his brow, but Sami suspected this one came from his need for the glasses. She was willing to bet he despised them because they gave visible expression to an irritating weakness. A man like Noah might make allowances for weaknesses in others, but she doubted he tolerated them in himself. Propping the half-glasses on his nose, he read the ad aloud.

'' *Man between the ages of 25 and 40 needed to contribute his all in a brief romantic encounter. Will be well paid for his efforts. Required to produce positive fruit from aforementioned labor. Must sign contract that any and all results will be the exclusive property of recipient.* ''

''See? It's very tactful.''

''You mean it's guaranteed to draw every nutcase west of the Mississippi to your front door.'' He folded his glasses and tucked them away. ''At least you had the good sense to rent a post office box for responses.''

''Of course.''

"I hope you also required them to send a photo, a résumé and references."

"Yes, I—"

She broke off. Wait just one darned minute. Something didn't make sense here. It only took an instant to figure out what. *He hadn't seen the ad before!* She studied Noah with acute suspicion. He returned her look with a knowing one of his own, no doubt anticipating her next question.

"Come to think of it, I never received *your* photo or résumé. I'd remember if I had." Boy, would she have remembered. "So, if you're not here in response to the ad…then why are you here?"

"Babe contacted me after she moved into her apartment. She was concerned about you being all alone here and thought you might need help. I don't think she realized quite how much."

"Hey!" Sami frowned at the reminder that Noah had been sent by her mother. "Maybe we should start over. Who are you? What are you doing here? And how is my mother involved?"

"You already know who I am. Noah Hawke, in case you've forgotten. Babe hired me as a birthday present. I'm supposed to work for you. In the traditional sense, I might add. When I saw the others in the hallway, I assumed you were interviewing someone for the job your mother hired me to do. That's why I cut in line."

"And what job is that?"

"Man Friday. Personal assistant. Valet." He shrugged. "Take your pick."

"Thanks, but no thanks. I'm don't need that sort of help. I can take care of myself and all the other household positions are filled."

"Except for someone to help make a baby?"

The barb hit home. "That's none of your business."

"Funny. Not five minutes ago you were interviewing me as a prospective father."

"That was five minutes ago." She pointed toward the door. "Now I want you to leave."

"Certainly. I'll be happy to go back to Babe and tell her that you're no longer in the market for an employee." He paused a beat. "Should I offer her my services as a baby-maker instead? Perhaps that can be your birthday present in place of a man Friday."

*"No!"* He was being difficult on purpose. He'd also managed to find the one downside to getting rid of him. "No, I don't want her to know anything about this."

"She's going to find out one of these days. Or were you planning to keep her in the dark until the baby arrived?"

"I intend to tell her." Sami tried not to sound too defensive. Not that it worked. She'd anticipated opposition to her plan once word leaked out. She just hadn't expected it this soon. "But I don't see the rush in bringing her up to speed."

"What you mean is, if she finds out what you're planning before the deed is done, she'll do everything within her power to talk you out of it."

Sami grimaced. Noah struck her as the type of person who'd prove himself right more often than not. How annoying, particularly when it was at her expense. "She might offer her opinion on the matter." Loudly.

"Got it." His smile appeared far too smug. "Then I gather you've decided to accept your mother's birthday present?"

"That's blackmail!"

He folded his arms across his chest. "So it is."

She stewed for a whole two minutes. "I gather I don't have any choice?"

"None. I gave your mother my word that I'd do this job and I don't go back on my word. Not ever."

He was dead serious. Everything about him communicated that fact—from his set expression, to the implacable tone of his voice, to the tensed muscles ridging his jaw and shoulders. She considered her options. Maybe he wouldn't be so bad to have around. He appeared strong. Capable. Intelligent. Maybe he could help with the interviews. She brightened. It might be fun to have a personal assistant. And it would make her mother happy. That alone was worth the inconvenience of having the opinionated Mr. Hawke in her life for a while. They only needed to iron out one tiny detail.

"Will you do what I tell you?" she demanded.

"I'll be your employee, if that's what you mean."

As an answer, it left something to be desired. Amusement vied with irritation. "You haven't done this for long, have you?"

He eyed her warily. "What do you mean? Done what?"

"You seem to have trouble taking orders." Suspicion dawned. "Is this your first man Friday job?"

He hesitated a split second before a wry smile eased the hard set of his face. With that one change of expression he switched from cool and remote to dangerously appealing. "Is it so obvious?"

Well, good grief! It *was* his first job. "Now don't you worry," she said, exuding compassion. "I have every confidence that you can handle it. No wonder you've been acting strangely. You don't know what you're doing."

A dangerous light sparked in his eyes. "*I* don't know what I'm doing?"

"I didn't think so." She swept aside his concerns. "But that's not a problem. You can consider this on-the-job training."

He started to say something, then paused. "Does that mean you're going to let me stay?"

Did he doubt it? Poor man. "Absolutely. How can I turn you away knowing that this is your first job? You should have explained that right off. I'd have been much more sympathetic."

He seemed to be having trouble breathing. "Let me get this straight. If I'd been experienced at this, you'd have gotten rid of me. But because I'm totally inexperienced, you're keeping me on."

She beamed, giving his arm another pat. "Exactly. Tell you what, why don't you take the day off? Relax and try not to worry too much. You can start tomorrow." She walked to the door and tugged it open. "Now if you'll excuse me, I have more interviews to conduct."

Noah followed her to the door and checked the hallway. "Make that interview."

She gazed at him in confusion. "Excuse me?"

"Interview, singular. Not plural. Your prospective daddies seem to have taken off. All but that one gentleman who's climbed on top of your highboy." Noah slanted the man in question an amused glance. "You might want to reconsider him. He doesn't strike me as too promising a candidate."

She looked in the direction Noah indicated, her mouth

dropping open. "Come down from there," she demanded of the man.

He shook his head. "I'm not moving. Not until you get rid of that wolf!"

Sami watched in interest as Noah silently signaled Loner to back away. The two worked well together, their obvious attachment a delight to witness. She returned her attention to her final interview. "Okay, he's out of the way. You can get down now."

"He's harmless," Noah offered.

"Harmless!" The man gave a short, humorless laugh. "He chased everyone out of here. Growled at them, licked his chops, bared his teeth. If I hadn't climbed up here, heaven knows what would have happened."

"Exactly what did happen. Nothing." Loner dropped to the floor and rested his head on his front paws. Heaving a sigh, the animal closed his eyes and began to snore. "See? Harmless."

The man scrambled off the highboy, edged around Loner and scampered for the door. "Wait a minute," Sami protested. "What about the interview?"

"Forget it. I'm not that desperate."

The door banged closed behind him and Sami planted her hands on her hips. "Now what am I supposed to do?"

"I have a suggestion."

"What?"

"Find yourself a husband. Then you can make as many babies as you want. It's safer. And it's smarter."

"Oh, dear," an amused voice came from the direction of the front door. "Am I interrupting?"

Noah placed himself squarely in front of Sami. "You are, if you're here for the interview."

She banged on his back. Not that it made much impression. The man felt like he'd been constructed from steel rather than mere blood and bone. "Move out of the way, you crazy man. He's not here for the interview."

"Loner?" The dog lifted his head, sniffed the air, then relaxed again. With a nod, Noah stepped to one side. "Okay. It's safe."

Sami glared. "You think?" Unfortunately, Noah proved as impervious to her sarcasm as to her fist. Brushing past him, she threw her arms around her visitor, relieved to have a minute to recover her equilibrium. Her brand new man Friday was entirely too disconcerting. "Uncle Reggie! How wonderful to see you."

"Hello, my dear," Reggie Fontaine replied, affection clear in his voice. "How are you?"

"I'm fine." She grabbed his impeccably ironed collar, crumpling it in her enthusiasm, and gave him a quick kiss. "Where have you been? It's like you dropped off the face of the earth. I've missed you."

"I'm sorry, my dear. Sometimes business gets in the way of pleasure." He glanced at Noah. "Aren't you going to introduce us?"

She'd rather not. Unfortunately, considering her uncle's obsession with "proper" behavior, she didn't have much choice. "Oh, sorry. This is Noah Hawke. Noah, this is my uncle Reggie Fontaine."

Reggie's brows grew together as the two shook hands. "Hawke… Hawke… Now why is that name familiar?"

"You're thinking of Mel Hawke," Sami hastened to explain. "Mother's ex-fiancé? Noah's distantly related."

An odd emotion shifted across Reggie's face. "Is Mel

back in Babe's life? I thought that was over and done with."

Noah didn't wait for Sami to respond. "No, he's not back in her life. Yes, it is over and done with. And that's not why I'm here." He paused a beat. "I'm Sami's employee."

"Employee?" Reggie stared in surprise, his gentle blue eyes filled with a combination of curiosity and concern. "I *have* been away too long. When did this happen?"

Sami glanced from one to the other, sensing some silent, intensely masculine communication between the two men that sent prickles of unease chasing down her spine. "Just now."

"I'm a birthday present from Babe." He folded his arms across his chest and planted himself squarely in front of Sami's uncle. "Whatever Ms. Fontaine needs, I'm to give her."

Reggie lifted an eyebrow. "Anything?"

"Anything," Noah confirmed.

Sami squirmed her way in between the two men. An elbow to Noah's gut helped, though she suspected it caused more damage to her than to him. She massaged the bruise. Impossible man! "I believe you neglected to mention that part."

"You'll have to excuse the lapse," Noah replied in a distinctly unapologetic tone of voice. "We haven't had much time to go over my job description. I thought we could do that when I moved in."

"Moved *in?*" Reggie glanced from one to the other in alarm. "Do you think that's wise?"

Noah offered a smile as innocent as that of a fallen angel. It suited his dark attire and pale, silvery eyes. His wolf-dog shifted to sit alertly at his master's heels, adding to Noah's dangerous appearance. "How else can I give her everything she needs?"

"Excuse us, please." Reggie grasped Sami's arm and pulled her to one side. "Have you looked into this man's background?" he asked in a low voice. "Is he safe to have in the house with you?"

"No, I haven't looked into his background," she answered patiently. She peeked at Noah, suspecting he could hear every word. Sure enough, an ironic gleam drifted into his calm gaze. "He was hired by Babe. If it'll make you feel better, I'll find out whether she's checked into his background."

"You know how much I care for your mother. But she..." Reggie sighed. "I don't mean to sound rude, my dear. But your mother's not the most cautious woman in the world. I'd be very surprised if she did anything other than catch a glimpse of Mr. Hawke's impressive physique and give her stamp of approval based on no more than her infamous instincts. Though why she believes they're in the least accurate defies all logic."

"She hasn't had the best luck with men," Sami conceded the point.

"Very gracious of you to state it that way, my dear. In my opinion, your mother's ability to judge character is appalling."

Sami privately agreed, not that she'd admit that to her uncle. As much as she adored Reggie, her mother received her first loyalty. "I'm sure she thought I'd need help now that she's moved out," Sami offered, hoping evasion might change the subject.

"Then..." Her uncle cleared his throat. "Your mother's involved in another relationship?"

"If she is, she hasn't told me about it."

"But that's the only time she moves out, isn't it?" Regret lined his face and dimmed the blue of his eyes. "So. I assume we'll soon receive invitations for marriage number five."

"Six." Sami touched his arm. "She loved Daddy more than anyone, Uncle Reg. You know that. No one's been able to replace him."

"But still, she continues to try. Not that my brother is easily replaced."

"Perhaps the next man will be different."

Reggie's chin firmed, as though anticipating a blow. "You've met him?"

"Like I said. If there's someone new, she hasn't told me about it." Sami made a face. "You know how Babe is."

"Yes, my dear," he murmured with a melancholy smile. "I'm well aware of your mother's eccentricities."

"Well, this is a new one on me. She's always waited for an engagement ring before leaving home. This time there wasn't even a hint. A couple of days ago she packed her bags, gave me a kiss on the check and breezed out the door. I only see her when she stops by to collect the mail."

"What in the world is that woman up to now?"

Sami caught her lower lip between her teeth. How could she possibly answer that? Babe was impossible to anticipate. "Perhaps she wants to live on her own for a while. She's using the Nob Hill apartment."

That gave him pause. He stood carefully erect, his spine military-straight, his shoulders taut. He tugged at his crumpled collar, focusing on a spot an inch above her head. "Your mother is not one to live on her own for long. I suspect we should prepare ourselves for the worst.''

''Perhaps it'll be for the best this time.''

For some reason that only depressed him all the more. ''We'll have to hope so. Your mother deserves happiness. Perhaps she'd find it if she didn't flit from—'' He broke off, a hint of color slipping along his cheekbones.

''From husband to husband?'' Sami asked dryly.

Anguish scored his face with deep furrows. ''I apologize, my dear. That was unforgivably rude.''

She patted his arm. ''Not rude, Uncle Reggie. Just honest.''

''Well, Ms. Fontaine?'' Noah interrupted. ''What's the verdict? Do you risk life and limb to keep me on? Or should I go now?''

Sami gave her uncle a reassuring smile before rejoining her ''employee.'' It bordered on the ridiculous to refer to him as such. She'd never met a more fiercely independent soul. His eyes had darkened in the few minutes she'd been talking to her uncle. They appeared harder, more untamed, blazing with a coldness that sat oddly with such a passionate spirit.

''How can I refuse my mother's birthday present? Or refuse you the chance at your first man Friday position?'' she asked lightly. ''You understand that I'll need references and a copy of your résumé?''

''Otherwise I'll be forced to put my foot down,'' Reggie explained in a no-nonsense voice.

''That's not a problem.''

''When will it be convenient to move in?''

Before he could respond, a pint-size boy burst through the door. ''Hey, Sami! You oughta see the car out front. It must take up a whole block. And there's this great big guy standing there. He's wearing a uniform and every-thing.''

"Hey, Pudge," Sami greeted her helper. "You're late. You didn't get another detention at school, did you?''

"Nah. I've been outside helpin'. You're the one who's late. Oh!" He snapped his fingers. "I almost forgot. You better come quick. That's what I come to tell you.''

"I believe this is my cue to leave," Reggie announced.

"Oh, no," Sami protested. "Must you? Can't you stay for dinner?''

He slid a quick glance in Noah's direction. "Not this time, I'm afraid. But we'll make arrangements to get together soon.''

"Promise?''

"I always keep my promises, my dear. You know that.''

"Is that car yours?" Pudge interrupted. "That big one out front?''

Reggie smiled in amusement. "Indeed, it is, young man.''

"And the giant, too? Does he belong to you?''

"He's my driver.''

"Wow.''

"Pudge?" Sami cut in. "You mentioned a problem?''

"Oh, right. You better get out back fast. All hell's breakin' loose.''

"Pudge!''

The boy sighed. "It just don't sound right to say all heck's breakin' loose. And besides, that's *not* what's going on.''

Reggie gave Sami's cheek a quick kiss. "We'll talk soon, yes?"

"Of course," she confirmed absently. *What in the world had happened?* "Any day you're free is fine."

"My dear—" Reggie broke off and shook his head with a rueful smile. "Forget it. Another time."

Something in his voice snagged her attention. "Uncle Reggie?"

"Never mind. We'll catch up later." Giving her a final hug, he made his way to the front door and left.

"What's the problem, Pudge?" Noah asked, his watchful gaze drifting from the boy to Sami. "Perhaps I can help."

Help? Not good. Not good at all. Noah had a most unfortunate character flaw. He liked to be in charge. This was definitely one situation she preferred to handle herself. "I can take care of it, no problem," she hastened to say. "You were going to relax for the rest of the day, remember? You don't start work until tomorrow."

He cocked an eyebrow. "Do I look like I need to rest?" He didn't give her a chance to answer. "Why don't I watch, so I get an idea of normal procedures around here?"

Pudge tugged on her arm. "Hurry!"

Sami blew wispy curls from her eyes. She had the distinct impression she'd run out of choices. Noah intended to follow her outside whether she wanted him to or not. "Okay, fine. Just don't scare anybody."

Silver-gray eyes impaled her. "Scare anybody? What does that mean?"

Sami planted her hands on her hips. "You can be very scary, in case you didn't know. And I'd rather you didn't upset anyone by saying something provocative or bulging your muscles at them or giving them that look of yours.''

"What look?''

Pudge danced from foot to foot. ''If you don't come now, they're going to kill each other,'' he warned.

Noah placed himself in front of Sami, once again. "Not while I'm around to stop it.''

She started to shove him out of her path, then thought better of it. Skirting him, she shot a quick glare over her shoulder. "*That* look, Tarzan.''

# CHAPTER THREE

SAMI headed down the hallway toward the back of the house, Pudge at her side. Even though she couldn't hear Noah's footsteps, she could feel him following her. How odd. Every sense she possessed remained alert to his presence—an odd warmth tracing a path the length of her spine, the suggestion of a delicious, alien scent tickling her nose, a quiver deep in her belly spreading heat throughout her body.

Who the heck was this man and why had Babe hired him? He didn't strike Sami as the employee type. He wasn't the least deferential. Nor did he take well to direction. In fact, she'd already discovered that he gave orders far better than he took them. And he'd admitted that this was his first assistant's job.

It brought her right back to her original question. Why was he here? The instant she found herself alone, she'd track down Babe and get some answers. Then she'd decide whether to enjoy her birthday present or exchange it for another model and brand.

Opening a door off the kitchen, she led the way outside to a small building. It had once been a garage, but when Widget and Pudge had come to live with her, she'd converted the ground floor into general-purpose rooms and the second story into a private apartment for her newfound friends. ''Now everybody stay calm, all right?''

"You don't know what's going on in there, or you wouldn't say that," Pudge warned.

Sami sighed. "Great. Just great."

"Why don't I go first?" Noah suggested.

Before she could formulate an argument, he opened the door and led the way into utter bedlam. Immediately, he placed himself between her and the others in the room in a manner similar to when Uncle Reggie had arrived. It was sweetly protective, but annoying. She peeked around him and groaned. Two women were arguing at the top of their lungs in two different languages while children ran around the huge room laughing and screaming. Music blared from a huge boom box and clothes were strewn from one end of the room to the other. A third woman sat huddled in a corner, looking totally miserable.

Sami stared, openmouthed. What in the world? "What is going on?" she demanded. Not that anyone listened. "Hey!"

"May I?" Noah asked.

Since her way wasn't working, she nodded. "Sure. Why not?"

He glanced at his dog and made a quick hand gesture. With a sharp bark, the dog burst into the room, amazingly graceful despite his limp, and swiftly corralled the children off to one side. The din lessened only slightly. A shrill whistle took care of the rest. A hush descended. The women turned and stared at Noah and Sami, while the children grouped around the dog, exclaiming in delight.

"You have a problem, ladies?" he asked.

They rushed him en masse, each trying to explain her particular concern. To Sami's amazement, holding up his hand brought instant silence. Now why hadn't that ever worked for her? "One at a time, please."

The oldest of the women, Daria, slapped her hands on her hips, switching from Spanish to English. "The schedule's gone and we can't agree on what needs to be done when."

"Where's Rosie?" Sami asked. "She should have a copy."

"Rosie has a doctor's appointment." Daria gestured toward the cluster of children. "So we don't have no one to watch the kids. I'm trying to pick an outfit for Widget, but Carmela say she have to do the makeup and hair."

Sami winced. Oh, dear. A rainbow of colors covered Widget's thin face and her hair had been poofed into a teased mass that swamped her features. The poor girl appeared close to tears.

Pudge shook his head in disgust. "See what they did to my sister? How's she supposed to get a job when she looks like some sorta freak?"

"Widget, why don't you go in the bathroom and wash up," Sami suggested. "Since we don't have anyone to watch the children, we can work on your hair and makeup another time. This might be a better day to put together your résumé. Don't you think?"

Sheer relief eased the tension in Widget's expression. "I'd like that," she murmured.

"I thought you might. Go to the computer room once you've cleaned up and you can work on that."

Daria spoke up again. "Good idea 'cept Leonard is runnin' an hour late. There's nobody to help with that crazy computer."

Sami swung around to face Noah. "Do you know anything about computers and résumés?"

"I gather you don't?"

"It's not my strong point, no. And don't look so superior. I could learn if I put my mind to it. I just haven't chosen to—"

"Maybe we shouldn't take that thought any further," he suggested gently.

She grimaced. "Maybe you're right. Let's stick to Widget. Are you able to help her or not?"

"I suspect I can muddle through."

"Great." She switched her attention to the women. "Okay, Daria? Why don't you choose some suitable clothes for Widget. Since she's not planning to work as an exotic dancer or fortune teller, we want simple and professional. I know I'm a fine one to talk, but keep the colors to a minimum." Next she turned to Carmela. "Since Rosie's unavailable, would you take care of the children?"

"No problem."

"Fantastic." She addressed Noah once again. "That brings us back to you. The computer room is this way."

"Why don't you also explain what's going on," he suggested.

"Sure." She saved her explanation until they were out of earshot. "Daria and Carmela are relatives of my housekeeper, Rosie. When I learned they were looking for jobs, I hired them to help Widget. Well, and Rosie, too, since she's due to give birth next month."

"Help Widget do what?"

"Get a job."

Noah took a minute to work through that one. "You hired two women to help another woman get a job?"

"Exactly."

"Why not just hire Widget?"

For a smart man, he certainly had trouble following simple logic—at least, her brand of simple logic. "Because Daria and Carmela needed jobs, too."

"You've lost me."

Sami released her breath in an impatient sigh. "None of them are mainstream enough for most placement services. Daria's husband died, leaving her with four children to raise. Carmela had her two babies when she wasn't much more than a child herself and is in the middle of taking adult education classes to earn her high school equivalency diploma."

"Those are their children running around?"

"Right. Having the children here while they work allows them to earn a living without the added expense of daycare. And since none of them has ever held down a real job…" She trailed off with a shrug.

"I see why they'd be perfect to help Widget," he muttered. "What sort of names are Widget and Pudge, by the way?"

"The ones they answer to," she replied evenly. "When they decide to use their given names, we'll call them by those instead. Do you have a problem with that?"

He took a deep breath and slowly released it. "I'm sorry, Sami. That was rude of me."

"No harm done, though I'd appreciate it if you'd hold the sarcasm to a minimum, especially around the women. They're doing the best they can under difficult circumstances and I don't want you to accidentally undermine their self-confidence."

"You're right. I apologize again."

There was no mistaking his sincerity and she forgave him on the spot. He'd been thrown into a peculiar situation and she could afford to excuse the occasional lapse of judgment on his part. Considering the frequency of her own lapses, no doubt he'd return the favor soon enough.

She smiled reassuringly. "Apology accepted."

"You were saying you hired Carmela and Daria to help Widget get a job?" he prompted.

"Yes. Without training, her prospects are pretty grim. She couldn't even afford proper clothing for a job interview."

"Which explains the wardrobe in the other room."

"Right. Even with the appropriate clothing, there's still a lot to be done. She doesn't know what to say or do during an interview. She's totally intimidated by the mere prospect of applying for a job."

"So, you're educating her on those points."

"Yup."

"You're providing clothing and teaching her how to fix her hair and makeup and helping her put together a résumé. I gather that's not the extent of it?"

"Not quite. I guess you could call Widget a joint project. I'm training her. Daria's in charge of wardrobe. Carmela works on her appearance."

"At the risk of offending you again, you might want to consider giving Carmela lessons, too."

Sami chuckled. "She did get a little overenthusiastic with her paintbox, didn't she?"

"Nicely put. I assume Leonard is in charge of résumés?"

"And giving Widget practice interviews. She's very shy. So far we haven't gotten her to speak above a whisper. But I have confidence we'll make a breakthrough soon.''

"Maybe I can help with that.''

"Really?''

She touched his arm without thinking and the muscles bunched beneath her fingertips, communicating an instant tension. Awareness filled her, an awareness she had no business feeling. Why had her mother hired someone so attractive? Couldn't she have chosen someone older…or less well put together…or ugly? Ugly would have helped a lot. Maybe. Or it would have right up until he fixed those silver-gray eyes on her and spoken in that smoky-dark voice. Then she'd have tumbled every bit as hard.

Her eyes widened. Tumbled? Hard? Oh, no. No, no, no. Thoughts of that sort could only get her into serious trouble.

She snatched her hand away from his arm and shoved open the door to the computer room. "Well,'' she announced brightly. "Here you are. Everything you'll need to help Widget create a résumé and practice her interview. And look! Here she comes now.''

"Sami?''

He was using that sexy voice on her again. She backed away. "I'll run along and check on Carmela and Daria and make sure Loner hasn't eaten any of the kids.'' She pasted a grin on her face. "That's a joke, by the way. I guess I'll see you later.''

He inclined his head, amusement cutting furrows of laughter on either side of his mouth. "Right. See you later.''

She lifted a hand. "'Bye.''

"'Bye.''

She couldn't think of another blessed thing to say. Mustering every remaining ounce of poise, she turned on her heel and walked away. She felt him watch her each step of the way. She didn't dare look over her shoulder. Otherwise she'd be forced to witness his amusement growing to open laughter. How humiliating.

Sami managed to give him an entire five minutes alone with Widget before curiosity compelled her to peek into the computer room. Widget was seated at the computer, cautiously pecking at the keys while Noah stood behind her, watching, his glasses perched on the tip of his nose. Every once in a while, she'd glance over her shoulder and smile timidly. He'd made quite an impact, Sami noted, pleased. But then, he'd made quite an impact on her, as well. Considering she'd been ready and all too willing to father a child with him... Yeah, she'd call that an impact. For the first time since her preteen years, a blush warmed her cheeks.

"Problem?" he called to her.

Of course he'd noticed her spying. "Just wondering if you needed help," she said breezily.

"I have everything under control."

"He's wonderful," Widget confessed shyly. "He said I could practice on him."

Sami's brows jerked upward. "Practice?"

A knowing look gleamed in Noah's eyes. "Her interview. I'm going to play the part of a prospective employer."

"Oh." How did she phrase her next question without giving insult? "Do you know what sort of questions to ask?"

"I think I can manage. After all, I had you as an example."

Cute. "You're supposed to make it tough on Widget. She needs to be prepared for anything."

"Got it."

She stepped into the room. "Really grill her. Force her to stand up for herself so she learns not to be intimidated."

"I understand."

"Perhaps I should—"

In one smooth movement, Noah straightened away from the computer and pocketed his glasses. "Excuse me a moment," he said, offering Widget a smile that brought an attractive glow to her face. He reached Sami in three short steps. Grasping her arm, he ushered her from the room.

"What? What's wrong?"

"If you knew me better, you wouldn't find it necessary to check up on me."

"But you've never done this before," she protested. "I thought you might need help."

"Do I look incapable?"

No! "I'll admit, that's not the primary word I'd use to describe you."

"Do I seem confused over the parameters of the task you've assigned me?"

She cleared her throat. "No, you don't look confused." She shot him a quick glance. "Annoyed, perhaps. But not confused."

"Can you see me playing the part of a tough employer?"

"As a matter of fact, I can."

"Then why would you think I might need help?"

He had her with that one. "Because you're new

around here.'' She seized on the first excuse she happened upon.

"I see.''

No he didn't. She might be slow in some areas, but
his ironic tone didn't escape her attention. She wriggled
in his grasp and he instantly released her, folding his
arms across his chest. Despite his air of detachment, she
suspected emotion smoldered just beneath the surface.
She couldn't remember a time when she'd been this unnerved by someone. Even the toughest individual melted
beneath her smile. But Noah was different. Very different.

"Since I haven't seen *your* résumé, I wouldn't know
what you can do and what you can't.'' She warmed to
her theme. "It's only natural that I'd want to check up
on you. Make sure you're not having any trouble.''

"Ms. Fontaine?''

"Make it Sami. No one ever—''

"Ms. Fontaine.''

She swallowed. When had their roles reversed? She
could have sworn she was supposed to be the employer.
Unfortunately, the icy way he said her name had her
snapping to attention like the greenest of employees.
"Yes?'' By sheer dint of will she managed to swallow
the "Yes, sir?'' his tone inspired.

"If I tell you I can handle it, will you trust me?''

"Absolutely,'' seemed the smartest response.

"I'm going back in the computer room now.''

"You don't want me to come in again, do you?''

He actually smiled, a delicious curve of broad lips.
She stared, fascinated. "Wise decision.'' With that, he
turned and reentered the computer room, closing the
door firmly behind him.

Sami slumped against the wall. "Oh, dear," she murmured. "I am in serious trouble."

"Well? Did she buy your story?" Babe demanded.

Noah sighed. "She bought it. Not that it'll do any good."

"What do you mean?"

"There are too many people with free access to the house." He folded clothing into his duffel bag, holding the receiver to his ear with a lifted shoulder. "That makes the situation much more difficult to control."

"Oh. You mean Sami's work project. I wouldn't worry about that. I can't believe the women my daughter's helping would want to harm her."

"Under the circumstances, I'd rather not rule anyone out." He hesitated, wishing he were free to mention Sami's other "work project," but knowing full well he couldn't. It wouldn't be professional. Nor would it be ethical. "Babe, let's contact the authorities. If Sami were some quiet, stay-at-home type, I'd have a chance of protecting her. But she's—"

She was a shooting star. A blaze of sunshine. A pallet of vibrant colors. From the mop of gleaming curls spilling into light green eyes, to the infectious amusement that underlined her every word, to the wide, plump mouth he longed to taste, she plucked at him like an energetic whirlwind, turning his logic upside down. What would she do if he gave in to the attraction stirring between them and kissed her? Laugh, no doubt. From what he'd observed she laughed at everything. He could imagine taking the generous fullness of her lips, feeling them part beneath his, sharing the warmth of her breath as amused enjoyment shifted to passion.

His gut tightened. She defied logic, forcing him to acknowledge emotions he'd be better off suppressing. These next few weeks were going to be a problem. A serious problem.

"You *can't* involve anyone else." Babe's adamant voice cut through the line. "Are you still there, Noah? You promised to keep this between the two of us. And as much as I hate reminding you, you owe me."

"Yeah, right." But he'd never thought she'd call that debt due. "Fine. I'll give it two weeks, Babe. If we haven't discovered who sent the note by then, I'm calling the cops. Got it?"

"Fine." Laughter remarkably similar to Sami's sounded in his ear. "That'll give me plenty of time to figure out a new angle."

Aw, hell. These Fontaine women were going to run him ragged. "What new angle?"

"To keep you doing what I want."

He sighed. "Not a chance, lady."

"Oh, Noah. You know I always get my way."

"Not always," he reminded.

"You'd be surprised." A hint of anxiety crept into her voice. "You're not going to go back on your word, are you? You've always put such a premium on honor. That's how I knew I could trust you."

"You can still trust me," he reassured. "I won't go back on my word. But I don't like this, Babe. By giving you what you want, I'm forced to lie to Sami. What's the point in keeping my word, if I have to lie? There's nothing honorable in that."

"If you give me a couple of days I can rationalize it for you."

He laughed in spite of himself. "I don't doubt that for a minute."

"Thanks for calling, Noah. Keep me updated, all right?"

"Count on it."

"And take care of my little girl."

"She's not so little," he felt obligated to mention.

Another bubbly laugh exploded in his ear. "I wondered if you'd notice." She hesitated, then said, "It won't work out between you two. I don't have to tell you that, do I?"

"What won't work?" It was a stupid question, a foolish one. One he regretted asking the minute he'd opened his mouth.

"You and Sami. You're about as opposite as night and day."

And he could guess which she considered him. She'd nailed him with her description, but that didn't stop him from pursuing the subject. "As I recall whenever night meets day, it can be quite spectacular."

"She'll burn you, Noah," Babe said softly. "Sami's not a forever-type woman any more than I am."

And that said it all. "Maybe I'm not after forever."

"Sure you are. It's part of your personality. Trust me. If there's one thing I know, it's men."

He could successfully argue that point, but it would involve more explanations than he cared to offer. He tossed his toiletry kit on top of his clothes. What the hell was he doing discussing Sami like this with her mother? He didn't intend to have an affair with his client's daughter—especially since Sami also considered herself his employer. The sooner he took care of business, the sooner he'd have the Fontaine women out of his life.

Permanently. Obligations satisfied, case closed and the last loose end neatly tied up.

"I'll call as soon as I have any new information," he said in his most business-like voice.

"Thank you, Mr. Hawke. I look forward to your next report," she replied just as formally.

He punched the power button and tossed the phone to the bed, glaring at it. He didn't want to go back to Sami's. She was pure, unadulterated trouble. She was far too attractive, had an uncanny ability to upset his equilibrium and didn't have a logical, practical bone in her delectable body. And if ever given the opportunity, he'd slip that delectable body into the nearest bed and allow her hot, sunny passion to burn him to a crisp.

Sure, he might go down, but at least it would be in glorious flames.

# CHAPTER FOUR

"THAT was fast," Sami said in surprise as Noah walked into the kitchen, Loner at his heels. "I didn't expect you back for at least a couple more hours."

"Want me to leave again?" he asked.

Absolutely not! "You can stay." Perfect. She'd managed to keep her tone light and casual, without a trace of an "I want to jump your bones *now*" inflection. She glanced at the black duffel bag he carried. Now why didn't it surprise her that he'd chosen that particular color? "You're moving in for at least a month and that's all you brought?"

"It's all I need, unless you expect me to wear a uniform."

Yeah, right. "Do I strike you as the type of employer who likes being surrounded by uniforms?"

He shrugged, an easy movement of his shoulders that stretched his black shirt across impressively broad shoulders. "Just checking."

"Are you hungry?" She gestured to the plate of fruit and vegetables she'd been munching. "Would you like something to eat?"

"I ate before I came."

"Oh."

How did he manage to disconcert her so easily? She'd never had that problem before. Good grief! She was twenty-nine years old. Again. By her age she shouldn't lose her composure around an incredibly good-looking,

62

sexy, appealing employee. She should be above that sort of thing. Instead, every time Noah shared her air space, her imagination ran riot, offering up all sorts of tantalizing possibilities involving hungry mouths and exploring hands and sweet words of passion. She dropped the carrot she'd been nibbling as though it had scalded her and leaped to her feet.

"Why don't I show you to your room?"

"Fine."

"You can unpack and relax for the rest of the day. You won't need to start work until tomorrow."

"First I'll unpack. Then we'll discuss my duties. After that I'll begin work."

"Oh, for crying out— Remind me again who's in charge around here?" His slow, easy smile answered her question and she shook her head, torn between amusement and frustration. "You know what? You're hopeless. Why in the world do you have to be so pigheaded?"

"I'm pigheaded because I want to unpack? Or is it because I've asked you to outline my duties?"

"Come on, Noah. You know what I'm asking." Sami gestured toward a doorway off the kitchen that accessed a steep staircase leading to the second floor. "Why do you feel it's necessary to start work today?"

He followed her up the steps. To her surprise, Loner didn't accompany them, but limped from the kitchen, toward the front hallway. No doubt he'd decided to explore his new surroundings.

"Your mother is paying me to do a job," Noah explained. "And I intend to make sure she gets her money's worth."

Sami held up her hands. Why argue about something

so ridiculous? "Okay, fine. I give up. If starting work today is this important to you, then feel free."

"Thanks. I figured I could put in a few more hours helping with your work project."

Which one did he mean? Her imagination ran riot again and she fought for control. "Now it's your turn to be more specific. Which work project are you referring to?"

His laughter rumbled in the narrow passageway, suggesting he knew precisely where her wayward thoughts had led. "I meant Widget. As for your other project, I'm hoping you're through interviewing potential baby-makers and it's no longer an issue."

"Oh, I am and it isn't." She glanced over her shoulder and flashed him a grin. "At least, for now. Fortunately, tomorrow's a whole new day."

The instant they topped the staircase, he grasped her arm, turning her to face him. Awareness hit hard. He had incredible hands. They were those of a man accustomed to hard work—long and tapered, strong and capable, yet with a light, careful touch. She couldn't see well in the dimness of the hallway and dressed all in black, Noah blended into the shadows. But his eyes stood out, clear and direct and piercing. She couldn't look away, didn't want to look away.

This man wasn't for her, she struggled to remind herself. She longed for a child, not a lover. She could even picture her son, a boy with dark wavy hair and silver-gray eyes, a sharp logical brain and a delightful sense of the absurd. For a split second, she saw into the future, a future bright with possibilities. It held a husband who loved her and a forever-after marriage. Children abounded, growing straight through to maturity. And happiness and security were hers for the taking. All she had to do was reach out and grab it. All she had to do was—

"Are you telling me you're holding more interviews tomorrow?" Noah demanded.

Her dream shattered, harsh reality rising up to replace sweet fantasy. "Of course." Her brow wrinkled in bewilderment. "Did you think I was going to quit because the first day went badly?"

"Hell, yes."

"Not a chance. I want a baby, Mr. Hawke. That hasn't changed just because your wolf scared off today's respondents. Not that any of this is your business," she added pointedly.

He expelled his breath in a long sigh. "Right." He released her arm. "Which bedroom is mine?"

"Here." She opened the first door off the staircase and gestured for him to enter. "I picked this one because it was my favorite as a child. I thought you'd like it, too."

The room was large and airy, with enormous windows overlooking the Golden Gate Bridge. She swept aside the drapes so he could admire the seascape. As the afternoon faded, fog had wrapped the bridge in a ghostly embrace before tumbling into San Francisco Bay.

He joined her at the window enclosure. "That's one hell of a view." His eyes narrowed and his gaze pinned her with a disconcerting sharpness. "But this room seems more appropriate for a guest than an employee."

She darted him a quick, mischievous smile. "I can put you up in the dungeons, if you prefer."

He ran a hand across the nape of his neck and tossed

his duffel bag onto a nearby chair. "It might be safer," he muttered. "How far is your room from here?"

The question caught her flat-footed. "Excuse me?"

"In case there's a problem. Where's your room?"

"Three doors down. It faces the bridge, too."

"Got it. In that case, this room should be fine."

She didn't dare ask why the proximity of her room had prompted the abrupt acceptance of his accommodations. It might lead places they were safer avoiding. She seized on the first topic that occurred to her.

"You know, when I was little, I'd sneak in here any time I wanted to be alone, even though it wasn't my bedroom."

"Why would you do that?"

"It had a window seat, which mine didn't and these drapes that I could hide behind." She fingered the filmy curtain, swamped by long-buried memories. "I'd stare out to sea and imagine all sorts of mythical sea creatures lived in the mist. Some days I'd swear I'd caught a glimpse of a giant fin or a mermaid's tail. Other times a great beastly head would lift out of the fog and blow smoke at me." She turned and smiled, praying it didn't look as shaky as it felt. "And I'd make wishes."

"What sort of wishes?"

His words were a gentle wash across a painful bruise and she made a point of turning back toward the view, struggling to keep the conversation casual. "Oh, you know. The usual sort of wishes children tend to make. Wishes that would fix whatever had broken in one's world."

His hands cupped her shoulders and his breath stirred the curls at her temple. "Wishes about fathers who'd left?"

"Yes." The word escaped in a painful whisper and she tilted her head so her cheek rested against the back of his hand. Strong hands. Capable hands. Careful hands. "Those sort of wishes."

"I gather they didn't work?"

"I eventually discovered that you can't change the past. It was a hard lesson to learn."

"No, you can't. But you can choose to move away from it and build a future."

She shut her eyes, compelled to confess the truth. "I told you my father left, but that wasn't quite accurate."

"No?" So soft. So gentle.

"Dad was killed in a car wreck."

"Aw, hell, Sami. I'm sorry."

"It was a terrible time. One day I was part of a family. And the next my family was destroyed. Babe and I..." She shivered. "We looked and looked. But we never found what we'd lost."

Noah remained silent for a long time. Then he squeezed her shoulders. "At least you knew what a family should be like. That's more than I had. I never knew my mother. She left my father when I was small."

Sami pivoted in his arms, her hands slipping around his waist in a gesture of comfort. "Did your father try and replace her?"

"My father was more intent on finding the quickest, easiest way to line his pockets." His chin dropped to the top of her head. "I suspect good ol' Dad could match Babe marriage for marriage. The difference is your mother was looking for love, whereas my father was looking for someone who could indulge his every financial whim. And trust me when I say Dad's whims were expensive."

"Oh, Noah. I'm so sorry."

To her relief, he didn't reject her sympathy. "We can't do anything about our past, Sami. But we can choose how we go forward. We don't have to be haunted by events beyond our control."

He didn't know the rest, the bits and pieces that would give lie to his statement. But she'd already said far too much. She'd bared enough of her soul for one day. "I'm trying to go forward. Can't you see that?"

"I gather that means you're still intent on having a baby." He didn't phrase it as a question. "Don't you think your child will miss having a father? You did."

She didn't dare look at him, too afraid she'd break down. She fought for control. Tears weren't her style. Laughter always made her feel far better. She straightened away from him. "Sorry, Noah. There's no room for a daddy around here. What my parents had was unique and when my father died it nearly destroyed my mother. I don't intend to go through what she did. But that doesn't mean I should live a life barren of children. I'm crazy about kids and I'm good with them, too. I've wanted to have a baby for as long as I can remember."

"And now you're going to do something about it? Why? Why now?"

Anger spurred her on. "Do you have any idea how old I'll be when my son or daughter graduates from high school?"

A hint of a smile touched his mouth. "How old?"

"I'll be—" She glared. "Never mind how old."

"That bad, huh?"

"The point is I want to be young enough to enjoy motherhood, not chasing my toddler around in a wheelchair."

His smile grew. "Somehow I don't see that happening even if you chose to wait a few more years to carry out your plan."

"I'm ripe *now!* In another couple years I might be rotting on the vine, all dried up and turned to a prune."

"You're right. You are ripe," he agreed, his voice low and husky. "Ripe to be taken advantage of. Ripe to be badly burned. Ripe for hurt."

"It's still my choice, Noah."

Before he could respond to that one, Loner burst into the room, a stuffed animal clutched in his teeth, his tail wagging enthusiastically. Sami took one look and started hyperventilating. "Mr. Woof. Noah do something! He's eating Mr. Woof."

Her expression must have warned him that panic wasn't far off. He turned and issued a sharp command. Loner set the stuffed wolf cub on the ground and backed away, his tail drooping pathetically. Noah crossed the room and gently picked up the toy, examining it. "There's a small rip along the seam of the ear. Other than that, it doesn't look like he damaged it. I'm sorry, Sami. I've never known him to do something like this. Would you like me to try and replace it?"

"No. It's not valuable." To her horror, her voice broke.

"Are you crying?"

Noah was beside her in an instant, gathering her into his arms. "Aw, hell. You are. Please don't cry. I don't do tears. I stink at them. I always say the wrong thing and manage to make the situation worse."

"Me, too," she said, the words ending in a sob. "I hate people who cry. Don't they know you should laugh at your problems?"

"Oh, damn. You really are upset. Please, sweetheart! Tears twist me into knots." He thumbed the dampness from her cheek and stooped slightly so he could peer into her face. "Tell me how I can make it better."

"I'm trying to stop. Honest." She took a deep breath, fighting for control. "Crying is such a pain. It gets everyone upset. Look. Even Loner is a nervous wreck." At the mention of his name, the dog shoved his snout between them, whining pathetically. It gave her the perfect excuse to laugh. "Good grief. He's in worse shape than we are."

"I'm not so sure about that," Noah muttered.

Sami dropped to her knees and wrapped her arms around Loner's neck, giving him a reassuring hug. "You're sorry, aren't you, boy? You didn't know how much Mr. Woof meant to me, did you?" He licked her face, cleaning away the last of the tears. She smiled up at Noah. Granted, it was a bit wobbly, but with luck it should pass muster. "There. See? All better."

He didn't appear reassured. "Are you positive? Would you like to talk about why an ear injury to a stuffed animal caused such a reaction? I'm a good listener."

She was tempted. Very tempted. "Maybe some other time."

He must have sensed he wouldn't get any more out of her. Giving a reluctant nod, he said, "I'll hold you to that."

She took the stuffed animal he handed over and crossed to his bed, sitting cross-legged on the end. "We seem to have gotten a bit off course." She deliberately injected a cheerful note in her voice. "What's next on our schedule?"

He started to say more, than shook his head. "Okay. We'll play this your way. For now. Next on the schedule is unpacking." He crossed the room to the dresser and tugged open a drawer. Returning to his duffel bag, he tossed it on the bed beside her and began removing clothes. "Were you planning to stay and watch?"

"I thought I might." She peeked in his bag, hastily drawing back as he returned for another load. "Good grief, Noah. Are all your clothes black?"

"It's a comfortable color."

"Why?"

"Because everything always matches."

"Oh." More questions bubbled up, questions she didn't have the restraint to resist asking. "Are you color blind?"

"Nope. I just don't do colors."

She chuckled. "I see. Afraid of committing a fashion faux pas, is that it?"

She'd actually managed to make him laugh, a delicious sound that filled her with warmth. "My secret's out."

Her nose disappeared into his duffel bag again. "And what's in this small leather case under your boxers? If it's a shaving kit, it sure is a weird shape. I didn't realize they made them triangular."

He scooped the case out of reach and tucked it away in his top drawer, his reaction almost as extreme as when she'd seen Loner with Mr. Woof. "That's none of your business."

"Oh."

He'd made a mistake, hiding the case away. Curiosity consumed her. What could be in it? Something he didn't want her to see, that was for sure. It reminded her a little of the gun case Babe-Husband #4 had. But that couldn't be. What would a man Friday need with a pistol? If she'd been a less trustworthy person, she'd have found a way to discover what the case contained and confirm once and for all whether or not her lurid imagination had gotten out of hand yet again.

She released her breath in a gusty sigh and gave it up. Spying wasn't in her nature. She wasn't sneaky enough. Nor would she be any good at making up a plausible excuse when he caught her pawing through his dresser drawers. The truth always had a way of tumbling out, even those few dark secrets that shadowed her soul.

"As long as you're invading my privacy," Noah said, "why don't we discuss my duties."

It wasn't a question. Once again she had the distinct impression that she'd lost the upper hand as his employer. How did he manage to do that? Maybe she wasn't cut out to be a boss, though she'd never had the least bit of trouble giving instructions to the cook or housekeeper or gardener. Only to Pudge. And now Noah. Who'd have thought after all these years she'd discover that she was a pushover at heart?

"Fine. Why don't we discuss your duties?" She offered her most innocent look. "Care to tell me what they'll be?"

He leaned against the dresser and regarded her with an unblinking stare as impressively intimidating as Loner's. "What's that supposed to mean?"

She shrugged. "Since you're my birthday present, it's a little difficult to know what you've been hired to do. Perhaps you should be asking Babe what she wants from you."

"I've already explained this. I've been instructed to give you whatever you want."

"I want a baby." Had she really said that? It was the truth and for some reason, she couldn't seem to help provoking him with it. "Were you offering your services in that department, too?"

His gaze never left her as he approached. Sami froze, unable to move or breathe. All she could do was watch as he walked toward her, his stride graceful and silent, his expression ominous. Even his eyes had darkened, the color the same dark gray of a fast-approaching storm front. It took every ounce of self-possession not to tumble off the bed and scamper out the door. Why did Babe have to hire someone so tall, not to mention so aggressively masculine? Why couldn't she have picked some sweet little old man who wouldn't dream of planting himself inches from her nose?

"Maybe I shouldn't have said that," she offered in her most conciliatory tone.

"Do you want me to take you to bed, Sami?" He'd pitched his voice low, the sound rumbling like distant thunder. It had the oddest effect, sending a desperate tremor straight through her, a tremor that took root deep in the pit of her stomach and spread outward in a swift wash of fire. "If you do, just stay right there and I'll join you."

That did have her tumbling off the mattress. "Noah—"

"Not ready to get down and dirty? Then why don't we start with something a little simpler?"

Sami swallowed, unable to resist the question he dangled before her. Who'd have thought she'd be so easy to bait. "Simpler? Like…like what?"

"Like this."

She waited for the inevitable. Because Noah's kiss *was* inevitable. The brief instant between his softly spoken "Like this" and his mouth joining hers lasted a heartbeat…and an eternity. When he finally kissed her she tumbled, every thought and emotion careening out of control. If he'd picked her up and dropped her off the TransAmerica building in downtown San Francisco, the fall wouldn't have been longer or harder.

It terrified her.

It thrilled her.

*Don't think!* she ordered herself. This wasn't a moment for rational thought, but a moment to appreciate each and every sensory explosion. His lips were warm and strong, capturing hers with a breath-stealing decisiveness. It was then that she made an incredible discovery. Noah tasted better than chocolate, which was saying a heck of a lot considering her obsession with that particular necessity of life. She locked her arms around his neck and indulged her newest obsession, one she feared wouldn't be easily sated.

She'd been anticipating this kiss almost from the minute he'd walked into her life and had taken over their interview. Considering his formidable appearance and forthright manner, he should have intimidated her from the start. At the very least, she should have found such a take-charge sort of man unappealing. Instead, she found him fascinating. He was a lone wolf dressed all in black, his silvery eyes blazing a path straight to her soul, his soft, rumbling voice seeping deep into the very fiber of her being. They were the perfect opposites, her vibrancy providing a blaze of aurora borealis color against his night-sky darkness.

His arms tightened, locking her flush with his deliciously masculine angles. Oh my, but this man had been well put together—large, powerful, and with a clear understanding of a woman's most secret passions. He muttered something dark and delicious, a suggestion that sent an illicit thrill racing through her. Her tongue tangled with his, their lips melding and releasing, before melding again.

She groaned, desire shivering through her. "Look at how well we're communicating. Maybe we should do this instead of talking."

"We were doing *this*. Right up until you started talking."

"Oh." She glanced at him from beneath her lashes, offering a half-sultry, half-teasing look. "In that case, are we going to argue? Or are we going to kiss?"

His breath feathered her face in a soft laugh. "I believe that depends on whether or not you're going to keep quiet."

She gave the matter a whole two seconds of serious consideration. "I think I can shut up if it means more kissing," she offered.

His head dipped downward, his mouth sealing hers. The heady lust-rush was every bit as instantaneous and intense as before. She stood on tiptoe, practically scaling him like a climbing wall. Her hands fluttered from his shoulders, down the definition of muscles across his chest to the flat planes of his abdomen. She didn't have the nerve to explore any further, though she wanted to. Badly. Instead, she lifted upward, tracing the strong sweep of his jawline and high-angled cheekbones.

Too bad he hadn't come for the daddy interview, the

wistful thought teased through her mind. He'd have been a perfect choice.

"Oh, dear," she murmured.

He drew back, his expression an explicit statement of intent. For a man who fought to maintain an air of implacability, she'd decimated it quite thoroughly. In any other circumstances she'd have relished untying his knots of control. But he wouldn't appreciate exposing his inner needs only to have them shut down. And that's precisely what she had to do.

"Um…Noah?"

"What's wrong now?"

"We shouldn't be doing this."

"That's only just occurred to you?" he asked dryly.

"You distracted me or I'd have thought of it sooner."

A hint of laughter drifted into his darkened gaze. "Are you always so easily distracted?"

"Not often," she admitted. "Maybe because I've never met anyone with quite so many distracting qualities."

He grimaced. "Thank you. I think."

"I meant it as a compliment," she hastened to reassure. "But that doesn't change one tiny—not to mention, pertinent—detail."

"You mean the tiny, pertinent detail that involves Babe hiring me to work for you?"

"Right. That one." Her fingers crept across his chest, intent on stealing a final caress or two. "You're my employee, remember?" She hoped he did, since she was having difficulty keeping that troublesome fact straight.

"I remember." He captured her hand in his, ending her tactile exploration. "I gather that means you don't go around kissing all of your employees?"

"Not all. Not even some. It's a definite no-no, I'm afraid."

"But it would have been okay to kiss me if I'd answered your newspaper advertisement?"

"Yes, though that's different."

"Because I'd be your…your baby-maker, for want of a better term? You'd be paying me for a different kind of service, is that it?"

Why did he have to make it sound so darned sleazy? She scowled. "That's about the size of it."

"And you don't see anything wrong with that? You're paying a man to have sex with you."

"I'm not paying for the sex. I'm paying for the same end product I'd receive at a fertility clinic. There's no difference."

"There's a big difference and you know it. I'm not even sure what you're doing is legal."

"You're being rude."

He lifted his eyebrow at that. "Try honest. Frank. Blunt. It's an outsider's take on the situation."

"I want a child."

"Try marriage."

She freed her hand from his grasp and folded her arms across her chest. "I don't want to marry. Not ever. I've explained that to you."

"Then try adoption."

"If I don't find the right man, I just might. Not that it's any of your business."

"It is when you proposition me."

Her brow crinkled in confusion. "When I…?"

"You asked if I was a full-service employee, remember?"

Oh. He must mean when she'd asked him if he wanted

to help with her baby dilemma. Maybe one of these days she'd learn not to say the first thing that popped into her head. It had gotten her into trouble more times than she could count.

"I wasn't serious!" she protested. "It came out that way because you offered to give me anything I want."

To her disappointment, he'd regained control of both himself and the conversation. "Perhaps we should discuss my duties and not veer off course into more dangerous waters."

She recovered her poise enough to smile. "It would certainly be safer."

He stepped back, giving her some breathing space. It only helped a little. He filled the room with the sheer force of his personality. If he'd actually shown up for her baby interview, she'd have chosen him on the spot, no matter how dangerous she suspected he'd be to her emotional stability. No doubt he'd make magnificent babies. And no doubt he'd be quite magnificent in all he did leading up to those babies. Not that she'd ever find out. Heck, no. From this moment on, Noah Hawke was strictly off-limits.

The next time they kissed, she'd tell him that, too.

"I have a suggestion," Noah said.

"A suggestion. Excellent. What is it?"

"It's about work. You do recall that's why I'm here?"

"Right. Work." She fought to focus. Why the heck did he have to be so darned distracting? "What's your suggestion?"

"How about if I stick by your side for the next week or so. That should give us both a feel for where I'll fit in. Until we come up with a specific list of duties, I'll pitch in wherever I can."

"Like you did today with Widget?"

He inclined his head. "That worked out, don't you think?"

"You were a bit on the bossy side," she mentioned cautiously.

"You'll get used to it."

Crud. "Don't count on it. I like things done my way."

"Another reason you're foregoing the pleasure of a husband?"

"Ouch. I thought we were going to avoid that subject."

"True." He picked up his empty duffel bag and opened the closet door, placing it on the floor. "Talk to me about Widget. Where did you find her?"

Another subject she'd rather avoid discussing. "She found me."

Noah glanced over his shoulder, studying her closely. She had the uneasy impression that he was busily analyzing everything she said and did. She found it uncomfortable in the extreme, as though every word, every expression came under intense scrutiny.

"Tell me more."

"You're doing it again."

"Doing what?"

"Giving orders."

"It's a natural talent."

"Cute." Something in his expression prompted an explanation she hadn't intended to offer. "We sort of ran into each other one day."

"Sort of?"

She wasn't going to get out of this one. He had a way of staring at her until the truth tumbled free. She couldn't even think of a good alternate topic with which to distract him. Now why was that? Going off on tangents didn't usually give her any trouble.

"Sami?"

"I don't want to talk about it."

"I'm aware of that. I'm also aware that you're trying to change the subject. That means the circumstances must have been unpleasant." He nodded in satisfaction. "I see by your expression I guessed right."

"How do you *do* that?"

He shook his head. "It's not going to work, sweetheart. I won't be distracted. Come on," he coaxed. "Confess. How did you run into each other? Did you have a fender bender?"

"No."

"Did you crash shopping carts?"

"Oh, please."

"More interesting than that? Okay, let's see... You both fell in a vat of chocolate down in Ghiradelli Square. You knocked each other over inline skating." He snapped his fingers. "I have it. You were both locked up in the same prison cell on Alcatraz Island. Am I close?"

"No, no, no and—let me think—*no.*"

"You might as well tell me. I'm not going to give up or let you change the subject."

"All right, fine!" Darn it all. "I met Widget when she snatched my purse. There. Happy?"

# CHAPTER FIVE

"AW, HELL."

"Darn it, Noah. I knew you weren't going to take this well." Sami paced the length of the bedroom. "That's why I didn't want to tell you."

"Shy little Widget snatched your purse?"

"It was an act of desperation." Sami paused in her tracks and attempted an encouraging smile. "Aren't you proud she actually got up the nerve to do something so decisive?"

*"Proud?"*

Sami winced. "All right, maybe 'proud' isn't the best description. But it shows promise," she insisted doggedly. "It means she's capable of standing up for herself when necessary."

"So what did you do when Widget took your purse?" He held up a hand before she could answer. "No. Let me guess. You didn't call the police."

"Of course not. I'm shocked you'd even suggest such a thing. Why would I do something so cruel?"

"I don't know. Maybe because a thief belongs in jail?"

"You think Widget belongs in jail? *Our* poor, little Widget?"

"Correction. *Your* poor, little Widget."

"Oh, no you don't." She stalked closer, her bracelets jangling in time with each bouncing step. "You can't back out of your responsibilities that easily. You've been working with her, too, which makes her ours now. And for the record, she only swiped my purse because she was starving and had a brother to care for and couldn't find a job."

"So what did you do?" He held up his hand again. "No, no. I'm getting pretty good at this. You took her and Pudge home and fed them."

Sami shoved her chin in the air. "I assume by your nasty tone that you wouldn't have?"

"Not a chance."

"What would you have done?" It was her turn to hold up a hand. "Oh, no. Let *me* guess. You'd have turned her over to the cops."

"In a heartbeat."

"How would that have helped her?"

"It would have kept her from stealing anyone else's purse."

"For your information, she hasn't stolen anyone else's purse. Her run-in with me was a one-time mistake. By helping out, I ensure she's training for a job instead of wasting away in a jail cell, miserable because she broke the law and even more miserable because her actions put Pudge into foster care."

Noah thrust a hand through his hair. His expression remained grim, but at least he wasn't arguing the point. "What's she qualified to do?"

"Not a blessed thing. Yet." She stopped him before he could make any more rude remarks. "But I intend to change all that. You'll see. She's going to be one of my greatest success stories. Heck. She'll be her own greatest success story."

"And in the meantime she and her brother live off of

you, along with Rosie, Daria, Carmela, their children and all their various relatives?''

"They work for me, they don't live off me. And even if they did, I can afford it.''

"Honey, my father would have loved you.''

Sami released a groan of exasperation. "I see what your problem is now. You're a cynic. You've lost all belief in the basic goodness of your fellow human beings.''

"I believe in their basic goodness. I just don't trust that goodness to last in the face of desperation or temptation or revenge.''

That stopped her. "Revenge? What an odd thing to say.''

"Why?'' He gave her a curiously intent look. "Haven't you ever known people who wanted to take revenge for a wrong committed against them? Or that they believe has been committed against them?''

"Absolutely not. Maybe we should talk about the sort of characters you hang around, instead of worrying about me.''

"So you've never inadvertently acted in a way that would anger someone?''

She shrugged. "Well, sure. I suspect I do it all the time. Take us, for instance. We've only known each other a few hours and I've already managed to annoy you any number of times.''

His expression lightened. "True. But nothing you've done would cause the depth of emotion needed for revenge.''

"Thank goodness for that,'' she said with heartfelt sincerity, "or I'd be in deep trouble.''

"What about someone you've know a bit longer?''

he persisted. "Someone you've managed to seriously annoy."

Good grief! "This is crazy, Noah. How did we get on this subject, anyway?"

"You haven't answered my question."

"That's because it's ridiculous."

"Humor me."

"Oh, for crying out loud!" She fell back on the bed, arms spread wide, and stared at the ceiling. "No. Are you happy now? No, I've never—to the best of my knowledge—done anything to anyone that was horrible enough that they'd want to take revenge. For your information, I like just about everyone I meet and they tend to like me, too." She lifted onto her elbows and fixed him with a pointed stare. "Although the jury's still out on you."

"I'm crushed." He approached, leaning against the bedpost closest to her. "What about the baby-maker you gave the boot to this morning? What was his name? Griffith?"

"So? What about him?"

"Aren't you worried that he'll be angry over your rejection?"

"Not at all. It was a tiny hit to his ego. He'll get over it." Deciding that turnabout was fair play, she asked, "What about you?"

She'd startled him and it pleased her no end. "What about me?"

"Have you ever gotten someone mad enough that they'd want to get even?"

He inclined his head. "Probably."

"You have?" She stared in fascination. This story she had to hear. "And?"

"And...what?"

"What did they do to you?"

"Nothing."

"Oh." She tried not to look too disappointed. "Why not?"

He slowly straightened. "Do I look like the sort of person who'd stand idly by while being attacked?"

"No." A sudden thought occurred to her. "Do I?"

A broad smile slashed across his face. "You look like someone who wouldn't see the attack coming, wouldn't notice when it hit and would probably try and make friends with the person afterward."

She grinned triumphantly. "Now there's where you're wrong."

"I don't think so."

"I do." She folded her legs beneath her and stabbed her finger in his direction. "And I'll tell you why."

"This I've got to hear."

"You're wrong because the situation wouldn't arise in the first place. I don't make people mad enough to want revenge."

"Come on, Sami."

"I'm serious." She ticked off on her fingers. "I annoy them, though it's never deliberate. I frustrate them, but it's sort of an amused exasperation. I peeve, I provoke, I defy logic. I even bemuse, bewilder and beset people." She grinned. "But mostly I get along with everyone."

His gaze had softened during her citation, a half smile curving the corner of the most kissable mouth she'd ever had the pleasure to sample. "You're just one of those people everyone likes. Is that it?"

"Yup."

"I can almost believe it," he muttered.

"Now that we've gotten that straightened out."
Scooping up Mr. Woof, she hopped off the bed. "Are
you ready to start work or would you like to have another philosophical discussion? Or are you going to take
the rest of the day off like I suggested and familiarize
yourself with the place?"

"Give me a few minutes to clean up and I'll join you
and Widget out back."

"Great. I'll see you there." She paused at the door
and offered her sunniest smile. "See how accommodat-
ing I am? Now how could you stay angry with someone
like me, let alone want to take revenge?"

Not giving him time to comment—she wasn't that idiotic—she closed the door with a good-natured bang.

*I don't make people mad enough to want revenge,* Sami
had said.

The minute the door closed behind her, Noah pulled
an envelope from his back pocket and studied it. He'd
found it sitting in plain sight on a table in her front
hallway. No doubt the contents would give lie to her
statement. There wasn't any question in his mind that it
had been put there by the blackmailer. It was the same
thick creamy paper and the same neatly printed handwriting as the one Babe had shown him. Whomever had
written it wasn't taking many precautions and if Noah
were allowed to involve the authorities, they'd have this
guy nailed pronto.

Fumbling for his glasses, he opened the unsealed envelope and removed the single sheet.

*Time's running out. Pay now or measures will be
taken. Soon.*

Succinct and to the point. The words sent a chill

through him that ate straight to his bones. What the hell
had Sami done to get this person so angry? Because she
was right. She excelled at bemusing, bewildering and
besetting. But she also was the sweetest, most generous
person he'd ever met. Even as she frustrated, she made
him laugh. And to hold her in his arms, to cover her
mouth with his…

He closed his eyes. Something about this note bothered him, but sharing that kiss with Sami had gotten him
so confused, he couldn't think what it was. As though
sensing his irritation, Loner whined in concern, shoving
his muzzle against Noah's hand.

He stroked Loner's ruff, infuriated by his inability to
think straight. *Damn it!* Babe had warned him. She'd
seen through him from the start, recognizing a man who,
like the wolf beneath his hand, would remain faithful
and committed to his mate, loving her for the rest of his
life. Noah had known for years his destiny was to remain
alone until he met the other half of his soul. How the
hell could he have suspected she might take the form of
a wary butterfly, garbed in a rainbow of sunshine and
determined to soar high and free? One, moreover, oblivious to the net poised just above her flyaway curls?

He set his jaw. Whether or not Sami knew it, she'd
just gained two protectors, both of whom would fight for
her against any and all adversaries. "We'll make sure
she doesn't get hurt, right, boy?"

Loner shook himself from head to tail and scampered
awkwardly toward the bedroom door.

"That's right. Let's go find Sami. We don't want to
leave her alone." He gave Loner a new hand signal, a
combination of two the animal already knew. "Guard
Sami. Do you understand, fella? Guard Sami."

He opened the door, allowing Loner to follow his instructions. Returning the sheet of paper to the envelope, Noah came to a decision. This was the last note he'd receive. If another message arrived, he'd turn it over to the police and to hell with Babe. Whomever was blackmailing Sami knew her. He was brazen in his approach. And he had access to the house. Noah winced. Either that or she'd neglected to lock the front door—a distinct possibility.

He didn't have much time and after his latest conversation with Sami, he doubted she'd provide any insight. Everyone liked Sami. No one would want to take revenge on her. He slapped the envelope against his thigh.

No one it would seem…except this guy.

"Uncle Reggie!" Sami exclaimed. "Perfect timing. That's two visits in three days. How lucky can I get?"

"Actually, my dear, I dropped by to speak to you."

"Can it wait? Noah's come up with a great idea and you'd be a perfect addition to our group. We're going to run through a practice interview session with Widget, Daria and Carmela. Usually we just work with Widget, but yesterday Noah suggested we try it this way so the others gain some experience, too. Rosie agreed to watch the children and I need you to catch any mistakes we make." She coaxed him with a smile. "You're so good at spotting things others don't. Will you help?"

He straightened his bow tie. "It would be my pleasure."

"I knew you'd agree. You're such a sweetie." She linked arms with him. "We're hoping if Widget has others there to encourage her, it'll give her some much needed self-confidence. We're trying to get her to speak up when she answers questions instead of whispering.''

"Widget is a bit shy.''

"But you always bring out the best in her, Uncle Reg.'' She planted a quick kiss on her uncle's cheek. "If you're there, I'm sure it'll make all the difference.''

"About that conversation—''

"Any time you want.'' Sami tugged on his arm. "Except for now. Come on. Noah's waiting. We'd better hurry before he terrorizes everyone and Widget gives up talking altogether.''

"Great. You're here,'' Noah said the instant they walked in the door. "I need your help, Sami.''

She pretended to preen. "Now why doesn't that surprise me?''

"It comes as a total shock to me,'' he retorted dryly. "Nevertheless, I thought it might be a good idea if you and I did a quick practice run-through. Widget and the others can watch and pick up some pointers.'' He inclined his head in Reggie's direction. "Good to see you, Mr. Fontaine. Would you be willing to critique our practice session?''

"Happy to,'' he said, taking a seat next to Widget.

Sami rubbed her hands together and approached Noah. "Great. If you'll move out of the way, I'll sit behind the desk and—''

"Not so fast, hotshot.'' He leaned back in the chair, looking entirely too natural behind the intimidating expanse of rich mahogany tabletop. "I'll be the employer this time around. I want you to play the part of the prospective employee.''

Say, what? "That's not how we usually do it,'' she protested.

"Which is probably where we've been going wrong. You're too nice as the employer." He didn't make it sound like a compliment. "So today you get to show us the other side of the process."

"Okay, okay." So long as it accomplished their objective, she'd be gracious and let him take charge. Besides, he assumed the role so naturally. "What do you want me to do?"

"Walk in like you're on a real interview." He turned his most charming smile on the three women watching the demonstration. "This time you'll observe while Sami and I show you how it works. Then you can take turns being interviewed."

"Have you ever done this before?" Sami stalled. "Been an employer, I mean. Do you know what to say?"

"Do you doubt my abilities?"

"Not exactly—"

"Good." He gestured toward the door. "Go on. Show them how it's done."

Giving in to the inevitable, she walked out, waited an instant and then opened the door. Before she could utter a single syllable, Noah cut her off. "You didn't knock."

"What?"

"I believe it's customary to knock on a closed door in an office setting." He addressed Widget. "If you're not shown into the room by a receptionist or secretary, always knock first. Sami's going back out to start over."

"I am?"

"You are."

"Noah's right, Sami," Reggie spoke up.

She groaned. Power and Noah did not work well together, especially when they were backed up by her uncle. She'd have to remember that. Turning around, she left the room and banged the door closed. It elicited another barked reprimand, one she deliberately ignored. Counting to ten, she pounded on the door before entering the room.

"I didn't say come in," Noah told her.

"Pretend you did."

He directed his remarks toward the women, but his silvery gaze never left Sami. "Not waiting to be invited in is a risky move."

"Being a smart aleck is a riskier one," she shot right back.

"Arguing with the boss is the riskiest idea of all. Oh, and one other tip." He offered Sami a bland smile. "Be sure you wear shoes to your interview."

Sami peeked at her neon-blue-painted toenails and grinned. "What if you keep misplacing them?"

"Then get a job as a lifeguard. That way you won't have to wear them at all. Okay, now you've been invited in. What's next?"

"I know this one." She approached the desk with her arm outstretched. "How do you do, Mr. Hawke? I'm Sami Fontaine."

He stood and leaned across the desk, shaking her hand. "I'm pleased to meet you, Ms. Fontaine. Have a seat."

"Thank you." She started to curl up in the chair, then thought better of it. Spine rigid, feel planted squarely on the floor, she sat with her hands folded in her lap and grinned at Noah.

He frowned. "Is that gum you're chewing, Ms. Fontaine?"

"Sure is. Passion fruit raspberry swirl to be exact. Want some?"

"Get rid of it."

"This isn't school, you know."

"You're right. It's a job interview that'll mean the difference between making your next rent payment or being put out on the streets. The gum goes."

She puckered obediently, the warning challenge glittering in his eyes too good to resist. She hesitated, trying to decide whether to risk the repercussions if she dinged him with it or if she should settle for depositing it dab-smack on the center of his desk. Before she could make up her mind, Noah flicked a single finger. Instantly, Loner leaped to his feet and howled, scaring the wits out of her.

Her instinctive shriek of alarm cut off abruptly. Uh-oh. She stared at Noah in wide-eyed horror.

He took one look and started to laugh. "Swallowed it, didn't you?"

"Yes," she croaked.

"Serves you right." He cast a speaking look at the women who were doing their level best to smother their laughter. Even Uncle Reggie was fighting back a chuckle. "So far you're getting a great lesson on what not to do. If I didn't know better, I'd say she was doing it deliberately."

"Hey!"

"Unfortunately, I'll have to assume that Sami makes a better instructor than employee." He glanced her way and lifted an eyebrow. "Shall we continue?"

"Maybe we shouldn't."

Not that Noah paid any attention to her. Slipping on his reading glasses, he flipped open a folder and scanned it. "It says here that you haven't held a job for the past five years. Would you mind explaining that?"

"I'm rich."

"Ms. Fontaine!"

"Oh, sorry. I gather you want me to make something up, right?"

He ignored her question and asked one of his own. "Delia, how would you have responded to that?"

She slanted an amused glance at Sami before answering. "I guess I'd have explained that I've been raising four children for the past five years while my husband worked. But he died recently and I need the job to support my family."

"That's a good answer, Delia. It lets your future employer know you're serious about working and not just bored and looking around for an alternate activity."

"So what do we practice next that I can get wrong?" Sami asked wryly. At her question, Loner released a gusty sigh and collapsed on the floor. Oh, dear.

Noah didn't appear any more enthusiastic than his wolf-dog. "This might be a good time to discuss our interview techniques." He picked up a pencil and tapped it against the desk. "Alone."

The women took the hint. They rose as one and scooted from the room, Uncle Reggie following behind, shaking his head. Even Loner trailed out the door.

Noah waited until everyone left before fixing Sami with a steely gaze. "Is this how you teach the women to behave at an interview?"

"Usually I'm conducting the interviews."

"So you've said." He tossed the pencil aside. "I thought you took this project seriously."

"I do!"

"So it's just me that brings out the worst in you?"

"You do seem to prompt an odd reaction." Many odd reactions.

"The feeling's mutual," he muttered. "I suggest we come to an agreement."

"I'm open to any and all suggestions."

"Let's agree not to torture each other unless we're alone."

"Torture?" she repeated nervously.

His mouth eased into a smile. "Maybe 'torture' is a bit strong."

Sami froze. His smile drove every thought from her head but one—the memory of his kiss. His arms had been so deliciously tight, his mouth moving on hers with urgent hunger, the taste and scent and feel of him driving her insane with need. He'd touched something deep inside and she didn't know whether she'd ever recover. Not when the memory of that one embrace kept slipping beneath her guard, haunting her at the oddest moments.

"Sami?"

She inhaled deeply, fighting to focus on the present and push the past into a dark, forbidden corner. What the heck had they been talking about? "Would you mind repeating that last part?"

He grimaced. "You're right. Maybe I should have said provoke instead of torture. We need to stop provoking each other during these practice sessions. It's not fair to the women."

"This next month is going to be a difficult trial period, isn't it?" For both of them. "Do you want me to return you to Babe?"

He stilled. "Is that why you're acting this way? So I'll quit?"

"No." She shrugged, experiencing a twinge of guilt. Maybe she shouldn't be so hard on the poor guy. He was just trying to earn an honest wage. "I pretty much act this way all the time. Sorry."

"I was afraid you were going to say that."

She leaned closer. "Trust me, I'll grow on you. Just give it time." She half expected him to offer a clever comeback.

Instead, he planted his hands on the desktop and leaned toward her until they were within a whisper of touching. "Honey, you've already grown on me."

Her eyes widened. "Aren't you going to say something rude?"

"Why would I do that?" His dark, rough-edged voice sank into her pores, touching places she'd guarded for over two full decades. She had no protection against him when he looked at her like that and it terrified her. "I like your sense of humor. I like your personality. And I'm downright crazy about your mouth."

She fought for composure. It would be so easy to get lost in his words, to believe what she saw gleaming in the silvered depths of his eyes. She moistened her lips. "But...? There was a 'but' to your comment, I assume?"

"I'm afraid so. These women need your help. They're not rich. They can't afford to indulge their sense of humor. These jobs are vital to them, as you well know. Otherwise you wouldn't be working so hard on their behalf."

She closed her eyes. "You're right. I don't know what came over me."

"Sure you do." Something in his tone had her eyes opening again, filling her with a painful awareness of him as a man. He closed the remaining distance between them and brushed his mouth across hers. "It came over me, too."

"We weren't supposed to do this, remember?"

"Then stop me."

"I don't want to."

"Neither do I." But he managed to, anyway. He sank back into his seat with a display of willpower she could only envy. "It's going to be an interesting month, wouldn't you say? And just so you know, I'm a 'no deposit, no return' employee. Babe won't take me back and I'm not leaving until my job's completed."

"Your job? Just so I have it straight, what's today's description?"

"Man Friday has a certain appeal."

"Yeah? Well, I didn't realize that a man Friday ever completed his job."

"This one does." His tone held a distinct warning she'd be smart to heed. "Babe only hired me for a short time. When I'm through here, you'll be the first to know."

His comment sent Sami sprawling across the tabletop to yank open one of the desk drawers. Grabbing a familiar-looking gold foil box, she sank back into her chair, ripping off the lid. "This calls for some serious chocolate."

"Do you keep boxes of chocolates in all the rooms around here?" he asked in amusement.

"Absolutely. I'm prepared for any emergency."

"And what's prompted this emergency?"

Her throat felt tight and she swallowed hard. "I don't like talking about endings," she finally whispered. "I'm not very good at them."

"Honey, you're the best."

"So what do you plan to do today while the rest of us are hard at work?" she asked with a tad too much enthusiasm.

"I think I'll stick around and see what trouble I can get into."

"Trouble?" Her guilty expression almost made him laugh, but he caught himself just in time. She was making this far too easy. "What sort of trouble?"

"I don't know. Do you have any suggestions?"

"Suggestions?" Her voice rose to a squeak. "Why would you think I might have any suggestions?"

He leaned forward until they were almost nose to nose and her pretty green eyes were fixed square on his. "Why, Ms. Fontaine. I do believe you're hyperventilating. Any special reason?"

"I— You—" She took a quick step back and thrust sunlit curls from her eyes, all the while shoving an outrageous lie through her pearly whites. "I have no idea what you're talking about, Mr. Hawke. None at all."

"I didn't think so." He flicked the tip of her nose with his index finger. "In that case, I'll see you later."

She cleared her throat. "Much later. Right?"

"Absolutely."

Satisfied that he'd be smart spending his day of freedom as close to Sami as possible, Noah deliberately kept out of sight for the next couple hours in case she decided to get rid of him with some trumped up excuse. He could guess what she had planned. He just couldn't decide what to do about it. Of course, he hadn't been hired to *do* anything—at least not about her baby scheme. But since her overall protection fell on his shoulders, he figured he was stuck with the job, especially since he didn't see an immediate end in sight.

So far, he hadn't discovered anything useful. No more notes had been left. He hadn't noticed anyone strange or unsavory hanging around outside the house. His mouth pulled to one side. Just inside. In the meantime, he was in the process of running background checks on everyone he'd come into contact with. He'd also turned the latest blackmail note over to an associate to see if fingerprints could be lifted off the stationery. Babe hadn't wanted to involve the authorities, but then, his associate wasn't an official authority. Until Noah received some feedback, he'd have to hang tough and deal with Sami the best he knew how.

Just after noon, his worse fears were confirmed. The doorbell rang and Sami pelted down the hallway in her bare feet. Snatching open the door, she hastily ushered her ''guest'' into the parlor off the foyer, the same room she'd used to interview Noah and the other baby-makers. It didn't take a lot of brain power to reach the most obvious conclusion.

The interviews had resumed.

Now what? Noah's eyes narrowed as he considered his options. He could walk in on her, though she'd most likely toss him right back out again. He could come up with some lame excuse to drag her away from her interview. That might work—for a whole two minutes. Or he could hang around in the hallway ready to rush to her defense should she call for help. Unfortunately, the door made an excellent sound barrier.

That particular detail worried him the most. She could stand in there shrieking at the top of her impressive lungs and he doubted he'd hear her. Another idea occurred—

one he didn't like, but suspected would be his only choice if he wanted to keep tabs on Sami and her "guest." It was an idea that would mean changing his job description from man Friday to groundskeeper and went against every code of behavior he'd ever held dear. But for Sami... He shook his head in disgust.

*Face facts, Hawke.*

He'd do anything for Sami, cross any line, break every promise. Whatever it took to keep her safe, he'd do. Once decided, he didn't waste any time. Heading for the kitchen, he exited out the back and circled to the side of the house. He could only hope that no one saw him skulking in the bushes and called the police. Or perhaps that would be the best thing for all concerned. Once he was arrested, the blackmail scheme would be forced into the open and his job would come to a fast end.

Babe would be ticked off, but at least Sami would discover the truth. Though he was willing to bet good money that what she chose to do with the information would defy rational explanation. Knowing her, she'd track the blackmailer down, bring him home and feed him. Then she'd train him for a job. Or hire him herself. Damn. The SOB could go from blackmailer to Sami's next man Friday in one easy step. She'd need a new employee, too, since Noah would still be warming a bench in the local pokey.

Crouching next to a prickly bougainvillea, he risked a quick look in the window. Good. He'd found the right one. Sami sat curled in a chair next to her guest—definitely a potential baby-maker if the man's ecstatic expression was any indication. Unfortunately Noah couldn't hear a word they were saying. As quietly as possible, he pushed at the window casing, amazed when it actually gave beneath his prodding.

If he were caught now, he'd have a lot of explaining to do, none of which would stand up to intense scrutiny. The chances that this man was Sami's blackmailer were next to nil. Still, Noah needed to be available to help his employer out of a sticky situation, just in case.

The murmur of voices drifted down to him, too muffled to make out clearly. Swearing beneath his breath, he gave the window another gentle push. It glided silently upward. Well, hell. That wasn't very safe. The minute he finished listening in on Sami's interview, he'd blister her about her lax security measures. Satisfied that he could now hear their conversation, he knelt in the dirt and pretended to weed the flowerbed.

"So… Mr. Sylvester, is it?" Noah heard Sami say.

"Make it Thomas."

"Thomas. I have a number of questions for you, if you wouldn't mind?"

"Not at all."

"You understand what I'm after?"

"A baby, I believe you said?"

"That's right. Do you have any problem with that?"

"Not even one," Sylvester assured cheerfully. "Only too happy to help."

The pig! Noah yanked viciously at a clump of weeds. He'd be only too happy to help, too—help good ol' Thomas out the door with an expeditious right hook. Sami, on the other hand, found his answer perfectly acceptable.

"Great. I just needed to make certain you knew what I expected. A baby, I mean. During my last round of interviews one of the men didn't understand my ad at all. And he wasn't very happy when I explained.''

''He doesn't sound too bright.''

''Oh, he's bright. Brilliant, even. To be honest, he had all the qualities I was looking for. He just misunderstood the situation. A shame really.'' A pensive note crept into her voice. ''He would have been perfect for the job.''

Perfect? Noah grinned. It would seem eavesdroppers did hear good things about themselves on occasion. So she considered him ''perfect,'' did she? Interesting. He found her pretty damn exceptional, too.

''I think you'll find me even more perfect,'' Sylvester asserted.

He didn't sound happy. Apparently Thomas didn't appreciate her complimenting another man. Noah could sympathize with that. He yanked free a few more weeds, feeling downright cheerful all of a sudden.

''We'll see,'' Sami said in a noncommittal tone. ''I have a number of questions to ask first.''

''Ask away. I have nothing to hide.''

Noah heard Sami's bracelets clatter and risked another quick look. She had her nose buried in a fistful of papers, no doubt her baby questionnaire. Jeez, she was gorgeous. Her hair had escaped her careful attempts to curb the wayward curls, surrounding her face in a halo of sunshine. From his angle he could see the curve of her well-rounded backside encased in form-hugging red cotton. Her figure hadn't escaped Sylvester's notice, either. If she bothered to glance up and look at his expression, she'd have slugged the jerk on principal alone.

''Okay,'' she finally announced, leaning forward to toss her papers onto the table in front of her.

Sylvester followed each delicious movement coming

from behind her cropped peek-a-boo top and it took every ounce of self-control for Noah to stay put. One wrong word and he'd be through the window, fist first.

"Question number one," she began. "If you had to choose between giving me a bright red rose and a cute little daisy, which would you pick?"

"Huh?"

Noah ducked down, smothering a laugh. Only Sami could come up with such an inane question. He couldn't wait to see how good ol' Sylvester handled this one. As distracted as he'd been by Sami's more obvious assets, he didn't have a hope in hell of concentrating long enough to pass the interview.

"Which would you pick? A rose or a daisy?" she repeated impatiently. "Weren't you listening? That's not a very promising start to our interview, Mr. Sylvester."

"I was listening, honest. I'd pick a... a..." He beamed. "I'd pick you a bright red rose. One that matches your tight red...er...*bright* red pants."

"Oh dear." Her breath escaped in a disappointed sigh. "I was afraid of that."

"Did I say a rose? Daisy! I meant a cute little daisy."

"You do understand that I'm not interested in marriage, don't you?"

"I understand."

Under other circumstances, his utter bewilderment would have been good for a laugh. Noah grimaced. Too bad these weren't other circumstances.

Sylvester cleared his throat. "But, ah... What does that have to do with roses and daisies?"

"Everything, of course." She snapped her fingers. "Here's a question for you. Does it bother you that I'm not wearing shoes?"

Noah groaned. He was willing to bet good money that question wasn't anywhere on those papers she held. She was probably still stewing over his comment during their practice interview session. Another handful of weeds strangled beneath his grip.

"No, I don't mind," Thomas reassured. "I think your toenail polish is pretty."

"I couldn't make up my mind which color to wear so I'm trying out the top three choices until I can decide. There's Shell Shock Pink, Insatiable Indigo, and Carnal Coral. The coral doesn't quite go with my red pants, but I never worry about those sorts of details. Which do you like best?"

"*Carnal?*"

"Yeah, that's the one I like best, too. Aren't those names a hoot? I don't know where they come up with them."

Her papers rustled some more and then to Noah's dismay, the clatter of her bracelets indicated that she was moving toward the window. He rolled closer to the stucco wall of the house, hoping she wouldn't glance down and see him.

"Okay. Are you ready for my next question?"

"I guess." Thomas sounded a hell of a lot less enthusiastic than before. "These questions are awfully strange. I can't quite figure what they've got to do with making a baby."

"They're vital," she insisted. "Now if I should select you over the other applicants, I'd like to get the job done as soon as possible. Do you have a problem with that?"

"Nope. How much of a hurry are you in?"

"A big hurry and by big, I mean huge. You see, there's some opposition to my plan."

*No joke,* Noah almost said aloud. Perhaps that was because her idea was the most idiotic notion he'd ever heard. Not that she'd agree with him.

To his dismay, she reached out of the window—her hand directly above his head—and plucked a hot pink bougainvillea blossom. Hell! If she dropped her gaze just a few feet she'd see him lurking beneath her like some sort of Peeping Tom. Why the devil had he agreed to take this job? He must have been crazy.

"You see, this new man I hired—the one who misunderstood my ad?" She plucked another blossom. "For some reason he's not too keen on this idea. Not that it's any of his business. But he could make things difficult if he chose."

"So fire him." Sylvester's voice sounded fainter than before. More muffled.

She sighed. "I can't."

"Why not? It's simple. Just say, 'You're canned, buster.' End of story."

Where the hell had Sylvester gone? Noah wondered. He sounded like he'd fallen down a well or moved to another room.

"I can't do that. He's my birthday present from my mother. What am I supposed to tell her? That I don't like him because he doesn't approve of my having a baby?" She sighed, her hand hovering in midair. "That would go over well. My mother would kill me if she found out what I was up to. But I really, truly want a child."

"And that's where I come in, right?"

Sami's hands flattened on the sill and she leaned partway out of the window, searching for more blossoms. If she poked her nose forward one more tiny inch, she'd see him. Worse, her peek-a-boo top was offering far too little "peek" and way too much "boo." Noah silently swore, forcing himself to do the decent thing and look away—but not before allowing himself one final second to drool. Desperate for a distraction, he fixed his gaze on an intrepid millipede marching determinedly out of the garden and into the grass.

Above him the bougainvillea swayed as Sami plucked another flower and he risked a quick upward glance. Apparently satisfied with her choices, she proceeded to stick the blossoms into her hair. If this had been any other time he'd have found her actions downright adorable. But forced to watch while groveling in the dirt, infuriated him. Why the hell hadn't he had the foresight to pull the damn bush up by its roots when he'd first gotten here and toss it in the nearest trash barrel? It would have saved him a truckload of trouble.

"Yes, helping me get pregnant is where you come in," she addressed Sylvester. "Maybe. If I approve you, I'd like to get started right away. Do you have a problem with that?"

"Not a one. I'm ready, willing—and if you turn around—you'll see I'm perfectly able."

She drew back from the window and Noah slowly rose from his cramped position, easing his aching muscles.

"What do you—" Her question ended in an earsplitting scream. "*Thomas!* What in the world are you doing?"

"You wanted to get started right away. Well, babe, let's go."

Noah didn't wait to hear more. One glance in the window confirmed his worst fears. With a roar of fury, he grasped the sill and vaulted into the room. Sheer rage took over and he charged flat-out toward the overly enthused man. "You son of a bitch!"

With a yelp of horror, Sylvester stumbled backward, holding up his hands before deciding they'd be put to better use elsewhere. "Who are you?" he cried. "What do you think you're doing?"

"Who am I? I'm the man who's gonna knock your teeth out." Noah cocked his fist. "As to what I'm doing. That should be obvious. I'm taking out the garbage."

"Wait! Let me explain."

"No need. Some things speak for themselves." In two steps, Noah caught hold of Sami's latest baby-making disaster and took great pleasure in slamming him through the door of the parlor into the foyer. At the sound of the commotion, Loner came tearing down the hallway, barking ferociously. Noah bared his teeth at Sylvester's terrorized expression. "Start running, buddy. It's your only chance."

"My clothes! You can't make me leave without my clothes."

"I can't." He snapped his fingers at Loner who howled in fury. "But my wolf can."

With a shriek of panic, Sylvester gained his feet. Yanking open the front door, he scrambled through it. Sami proved more generous than Noah would have been. She snatched up the clothes scattered across the parlor and raced to the door, tossing them onto the porch.

"And don't come back," she shouted.

Slamming the door closed, Noah turned on Sami. "Your turn," he announced in a low, dangerous voice.

"Me? What did I do?"

He caught her arm and ushered her back into the parlor. "Loner, guard," he commanded before closing the door. Releasing Sami, he schooled himself to silence and waited.

"You called Loner a wolf."

"Did I?"

"Yes, you did. Maybe you should explain that."

"Maybe I shouldn't."

She stared at him, her green eyes huge and alarmed. "And you're blocking the exit."

"I intend to continue blocking it, too."

"And...and you're scowling."

"That comes as a surprise?"

"Not really." She cleared her throat as she grappled for a different tack to use on him. "Boy, you sure arrived in the nick of time. Thanks for the assist. I think I'll be running along now. Okay?"

"Not even a little." For some reason he had trouble bringing order to the chaotic words seething in his brain. He finally managed to push them out of his mouth through sheer dint of will, though strangely, his teeth got in the way. Maybe it had something to do with the fact that he was gritting them so hard they were on the verge of fusing together. "That. Man. Was. *Naked*."

She broke into speech. "You noticed, too? Boy, oh boy, he sure was naked. Not a blessed stitch on him anywhere. I don't know how I could have missed him stripping down, but I did. Shame on me. I guess next time I'll have to pay more attention." She scrambled for something else to say and he waited her out, since it gave him time to recover his temper. Somewhat. "My goodness, it shocked the heck out of me."

"I don't know why." The words escaped in a roar and he fought to lower his voice, with only limited success. So much for recovering his temper. "It's clear he planned to offer an immediate response to your ad."

"I guess you could say he got his hopes inflated. But I noticed you took the air out of his aspirations." She winced at Noah's expression. "And I'm grateful. Very grateful."

"Not funny, Sami!"

"Don't yell at me. I don't like it."

"I don't mean to yell." He thrust a hand through his hair, tumbling the dark waves. "Damn it all! Yes, I do mean to yell. Have you lost your mind? That man could have hurt you. If I hadn't come in when I had—"

"You know, I'm glad you brought that up. You came in through the window, didn't you?"

"So?"

"So, what were you doing out there?"

"Rescuing you."

"No. I mean before that."

"Making sure you didn't need rescuing."

Her mouth fell open. "You were *eavesdropping* on my conversation?"

He refused to feel guilty over his slip in ethics, not when so much more was at stake. "You gave me the day off. I decided to spend it gardening." He stalked to the window and pointed to the pathetic clump of weeds he'd yanked from the ground. "See?"

She joined him at the window and peered out. "For your information that's mint, not weeds."

"Then it's a good thing you didn't hire me as your gardener."

"Were you listening in on my interview?" she demanded.

A hot surge of anger ripped through him. "You're not

turning this around, Sami. Be grateful I was there. I don't think good ol' Thomas would have taken no for an answer. What would you have done then?''

''Gone for help, of course.''

''Really? Let's pretend I'm Thomas.'' He took up a stance in front of the doorway and gestured for her to approach. ''Come on. To get help you have to fight your way past me. Show me how you're going to do that.''

She crept toward him, stumbling to a halt just out of arm's reach. Her face had turned so ashen he could see tiny pinprick freckles scattered across her nose. ''I don't want to try and get through you,'' she said in a small voice. ''You're not Thomas and never could be.''

''Do you think you'd have gotten past him any better than you could get past me?''

''If the interview had turned ugly, I'd have fought him.''

''I don't doubt you would have. You're scrappy, I'll give you that. But you're only five foot two or three. Let's be generous and say you weigh a whole hundred and ten.''

She started to correct him, thought better of it, and fell silent.

''Are you beginning to understand, Sami?'' He spread his arms wide. ''I'm six foot one and run a solid one-eighty-five. Now picture me naked and determined.''

''Oh, don't try and make me feel better!'' she snapped. ''You should have quit when you were ahead and I was scared spitless.''

He didn't dare follow up on that telling comment. He fought to cover his amusement by rekindling his anger. Not that it took much effort. ''You bring a stranger into your house. You tell him you want to have his baby.

And then you say you're in a big hurry—*and by big, I mean huge.*'' She started at hearing her own words repeated back to her. "I don't know why you're surprised or shocked or even mildly intrigued when he takes you at your word."

"You *were* listening."

"You're damn right I was listening! And by the way, what the hell was all that about roses and daisies?" He grimaced. Apparently digressing was contagious. "Are those the sorts of questions you asked all the people you interviewed?"

"Are you done yelling at me?"

"I'm not sure."

She planted her fists on her hips. "If you're through, I'll answer."

"Fine." He couldn't resist a final warning. "But, sweetheart, I swear if you ever do anything this foolish again, I will personally make certain you regret it." He considered the other two thousand threats he'd like to make and decided to save them for next time. Because there wasn't a doubt in his mind that there would be a next time. "Okay, now I'm done. Explain about the flowers."

"I was attempting to establish whether he had any romantic interest in me."

"Oh, I think he established that just fine."

"Not that sort of interest! Don't you get it? Roses?"

He shook his head. "I must be particularly dense. I haven't a clue what they're supposed to mean in relation to your interview."

"Red roses symbolize everlasting love. Men give them to women they're interested in courting. Or to express serious intent."

"No," he instantly corrected. "Men give flowers because women go starry-eyed over them and allow the sorry SOBs to get away with things they wouldn't otherwise have a chance in hell of getting away with. In case you're interested, men regard flowers in precisely two ways. One. They're an easy way into a woman's bed. Or two. They're an easy way to get out of trouble with a woman and back into her bed."

"You're such a cynic!"

"No, I'm a realist. And here's one more fact you can file away. Roses are only utilized as a last resort."

He'd gotten her with that one. "Why?"

"Because they're too damned expensive to use unless all other methods have failed. Trust me. I learned from an expert."

She stared at him, stricken. "Your father?"

"Let's just say I received quite an interesting education from dear old Dad." He dismissed the subject with a careless shrug. "Which brings us back to my original question. Why force your prospective baby-makers to choose between a rose and a daisy?"

"I wish you'd stop calling them that," she complained. He responded with a lifted eyebrow and she caved. "Oh, all right. I make them choose because if they pick the rose it means they're hoping to romance me. I don't want a romantic affair. I want daisies."

"You're not getting either one, sweetheart. All you're going to end up with is serious trouble. You were lucky. I managed to discourage Mr. Sylvester without too much effort. What happens if the next guy is more persistent?"

"You know his name?" As usual she'd gone off on a tangent. "How long were you under that window?"

"Long enough."

He watched as she struggled to recall what had been said. She even started checking off on her fingers, allowing him to silently follow along. First she'd asked Sylvester's name. Then she'd made sure he understood the nature of her ad. And then she'd told him about Noah. Granted, she hadn't called him by name. But she'd said enough for him to figure out who she meant. Best of all, she'd described him as "perfect." He waited for her to remember that vital detail. It took less than ten seconds.

"Oh, no!" Hot color washed into her cheeks and she closed her eyes with a groan. "Oh, no, no, no."

Noah leaned closer, not cutting her any slack. "That's right. I heard."

"You heard what?" she asked with a hint of bravado. No doubt she hoped he was stringing her along and hadn't actually caught that part of her conversation with Sylvester.

"That you thought I was perfect."

She covered her face with her hands. "Crud."

"Mind telling me what qualifies me as perfect daddy material?"

"Yes, as a matter of fact I do mind. That's between me and whomever I finally choose to father my baby."

No. She had to be kidding. "That's a sick joke, right?" he bit out. "You're not serious?"

She dropped her hands and glared at him. "Of course, I'm serious," she retorted. "My list of qualifications is confidential. You're just one of a…of a *slew* of possibly perfect daddies-to-be. Others could have the right qualities, too."

He fought back a bellow of frustration. "I'm not talking about your damn list! I'm talking about your plan to have a baby. I can't believe after what happened today that you're still intent on conducting more interviews.''

She dismissed his concern with a wave of her hand. "That was an isolated incident. It won't happen again. Next time I'll pay attention. The minute he starts unbuttoning or unzipping or—"

"I have a solution to your baby problem." He had no idea where the words came from, or how or when he'd formulated his plan. All he knew was that he was about to cross another ethical line. Cross? Hell, he planned to vault straight over it and several others, besides.

She eyed him warily. "What?"

"Continuing these sorts of open interviews is dangerous. Next time you could get hurt."

"I'm not giving up on having a baby!"

"That isn't what I was going to suggest."

"Then what?"

"I have two suggestions. Either go to a clinic and have it done in a safe environment."

"Or?"

He fixed her with a determined gaze. "You told Sylvester you'd found the perfect man. Why don't you consider asking him to father your baby?"

# CHAPTER SEVEN

"THE perfect man? But…but that's you," Sami sputtered.

Noah nodded, his gaze steady and unflinching. "Standing right here in front of you, sweetheart. Mr. Perfect."

She caught her lip between her teeth in an uncharacteristic display of uncertainty. "I don't understand. Why are you offering to do this?"

"Would you believe a whim?"

She shook her head. "Not even a little."

He didn't bother pursuing that line of defense. There wasn't any point. Keeping her safe was imperative, more important than any other consideration. To do that, he needed to sell her on whatever logical argument she'd buy. With luck, it would gain her agreement to his crazy suggestion. Not that he had any intention of following through with his offer. He simply needed to stall her—without arousing her suspicions—until he found her blackmailer. "Okay. Then, would you believe that I don't want you put at further risk?"

"Sure. I can accept that excuse. Maybe." She studied him anxiously. "There's only one problem. You've always been opposed to my plan. I find it hard to believe that your concern for my safety would outweigh your objections. There has to be another reason."

He took matters one step further. "Another reason and a condition."

"Oh!" Her bracelets jangled as he paced in front of him. "I knew it. What's the reason?"

"I want you."

Clearly, she hadn't anticipated him saying that. She stumbled to a halt and stared, wide-eyed. "You—"

"Want to make love to you. Yes." He lifted an eyebrow. "Don't tell me that comes as a surprise."

She swallowed. "Somewhat. And…and the condition?"

So far he'd been able to stick to the truth. He could only hope it would last. "You've said you won't have an ongoing relationship with the father of your child, other than sexual, that is. I can't agree to that."

"You have to!"

"The hell I do. What sort of man would father a child and walk away afterward? Is that the sort of person you'd respect? The sort of man you'd want to get you with child?"

For a split second her gaze softened at his phrasing. It didn't last long. Her jaw firmed, poking in his direction. "Maybe."

He couldn't help laughing, despite the seriousness of the situation. "No, you wouldn't. It wouldn't be fair to you or our baby." He made a point of stressing the word "our." She'd forgotten that aspect or pushed it from her mind. He intended to keep it right there in front of her, forcing her to deal with the issue. "If your plans come to fruition, we'll be parents in less than a year. Both of us. Do you really intend to shut me out of the experience?"

Hope mingled with apprehension. "What are you suggesting?"

"I want us to get to know each other before we go

through with this.'' Anything to delay her. Still, he chose
his arguments carefully, some deep yearning urging him
to bind them together with every word he uttered, forcing Sami to mate the two of them in her thoughts and
emotions. ''I want us to make certain our decision is the
right one. Once you're pregnant, we'll be committed.
Changing our minds won't be an option. So I suggest
we make very sure this isn't a mistake.''

''You'd like us to get to know each other?'' she clar-
ified. ''In what way?''

''In the usual way men and women go about establishing a relationship.''

''You expect to *date* me?''

''Would you rather I said I hoped to sleep with you?''

''If that's the truth, then yes.''

''I do want to sleep with you.''

Her expression hardened. ''I knew it. This is all some
elaborate scam to get me into your bed.''

''Getting you into bed was never the hard part.'' He
waited for the blow to strike before softening it. ''I also
want to know you as a person.''

''Why?'' she whispered. He'd never seen her so vul-
nerable and it tore him apart.

''You know why. There's something there, whether
you're willing to admit it or not.''

''Right. Sexual attraction.''

He shook his head. ''Don't lie to yourself. It's more
than that, Sami. Otherwise that kiss would never have
happened.''

''Whatever it is, I'm not interested.'' He could practically see her throwing up barriers, reinforcing them as
hard and fast as possible. ''I don't handle long-term
well. In fact, I stink at it.''

He changed tactics. "Even when it's perfect? You said you were looking for the perfect man to father the perfect child. Why are you resisting?"

"I don't mean perfect as in *perfect*." She scrambled for another excuse. "I'm searching for a man who compliments me, whose strengths balance my weaknesses and vice versa."

"Exactly. For instance… You might not do long-term well, but I excel at it." He ached to pull her into his arms. But she looked as wary as Loner when Noah had first stumbled across the half-starved, terrified cub. "I can teach you how. All you have to do is trust me, sweetheart."

"This is a really bad idea."

"Is it? Why don't we put it to the test?"

He crossed to the sitting area and picked up her questionnaire. He waited for her to say something or to take the papers from him. When she didn't, he pulled out his reading glasses and scanned the pages. There was a notation at the top of her list reminding her to ask for the applicants name, age and marital status. Next came her infamous rose versus daisy question. Then there were several dozen more questions, all neatly typed and printed. And finally, in the margin beside the questions, a list of characteristics were scrawled in what could only be Sami's inimitable handwriting—feminine and appealingly loopy.

*Powerful,* she'd written, *both mentally and physically. Calm. Logical. Patient. Must have common sense.* The word "must" had been underlined several times. *Kind. Generous. Willing to pitch in at a moment's notice. Protective. Loves animals. Owning a wolf a plus.* His mouth twitched as he read that one. *Strong, gentle hands. Looks good in black. Clear, direct eyes. Gray color another plus. Can kiss like a dream. Most of all…must understand the importance of family.*

It took a long moment before he could gather his control enough to speak. "This is quite a list."

"See? I really did have some good questions. And you doubted me. Ha!" She smiled in triumph. "That'll teach you."

He waited until her bravado had died before gently explaining, "I'm not talking about the questions. I mean the list you made beside the questions." He slipped off his glasses and tapped the papers with the earpiece. "Is this how you see me?"

Shock darkened Sami's eyes. Apparently she'd forgotten about the added notations. "The…ah…list?"

He held out the pertinent page. "Would you care to refresh your memory?"

She snatched it from his grasp and hastily read through it. "Oh. Oh, right. This stuff."

"Stuff?" Thoroughly irritated by her attitude, he tossed his glasses in the general direction of the coffee table. They clattered against the wood, before sliding to the floor.

Her shirt rose and fell, betraying her agitation. "Just me being silly," she claimed.

He wasn't about to let her get away with that. "So you didn't mean any of it?"

"Well maybe the part about the eyes. And the wolf." She cleared her throat. "Oh, and this little bit here about you looking good in black. I must admit, you do have a way with that particular color."

"What about the rest?"

She gave up, surrendering to the inevitable. "What do

you want me to say, Noah? That I think you're wonderful? That I think you exemplify all the qualities I'm
hoping to find in the man who will father my child?
Okay, fine. I admit it. Yes, that's how see you. You're
all that and more. In fact, you're I-Can't-Believe-It's-
True-Try-Not-To-Drool-When-You-Look-At-Him Mr.
Perfect. Satisfied?''

More than satisfied. "Then why are you resisting my
suggestion?''

''Because I have a funny feeling you're after permanent and I don't do permanent well. I change my mind
more often than my nail polish.''

"I rarely change mine.''

That cheered her right up. ''Precisely my point. We're
opposites.''

''It gives us balance,'' he countered.

''Not when I like taking care of people and you enjoy
chasing them off.''

''Only the bad ones.'' He gave her a little push in the
appropriate direction. ''Protective, remember? It was one
of the characteristics you appreciate.''

''Maybe so, but you're also logical.'' She made it
sound like a defect.

''Don't you think one of us should be?'' He indicated
the paper she still held. ''Honey, it's all right there in
black and white. Logical. Protective. Calm. Common
sense. By the way, I'm delighted you think one of us
should have some.''

''I've decided to scratch out that part.'' She snatched
up a pen, putting action to words. ''It gets in the way.''

''In that case, I'll try and keep common sense and
logic to a minimum. Would that satisfy you?''

''You're too overwhelming.''

"Correction. I'm physically and mentally powerful."

"Right. That part goes, too." She started to scribble over that, as well, then hesitated. "You're not going to give up on this, are you?"

He shook his head. "No. And I'll go one better. I'll tell you what I really think about your plan."

"Oh, please." Sarcasm rippled through her voice. "Don't keep me in suspense."

"You don't want the perfect man or the perfect baby."

"You're wrong!"

"Stop kidding yourself, honey." He hit her with his take on the truth. "You're hoping to create something better, to connect to something larger so you're not alone anymore. That's why you want a man who understands the importance of family. Because it's what you're missing in your own life. Well, I'm here to tell you that a baby won't give you that. But a husband and children together just might."

An intense yearning slipped across her face, almost painful to behold. "I don't think that's possible."

"You'll never know unless you try." He held out his hand. "Do we have a deal? First we'll get to know each other. If it works out, we'll consider having a baby together."

"And if it doesn't?"

"There's always the clinic."

"Oh, Noah. I'm not sure about this."

"I am." This time he did reach for her, pulling her into his arms. "Let me convince you."

She moistened her tongue in a way that made him think of hot, sweet kisses. Slow kisses, deep kisses, an endless slide of lips and tongue that drugged the senses and could only lead one place—straight to bed for a night of long, soul-altering passion. If he were smart, he'd walk out that door and out of her life. But he couldn't bring himself to do that.

Babe had been right when she'd warned him against developing feelings for Sami. They were total opposites. He played night to her day, her personality as sunny and warm and emotional as his was quiet and deliberate and rooted in logic. He provided a rocklike solidity for her fluidity, her enthusiasm flowing over and around him, as bright and refreshing as a mountain stream. And like a rock in that stream, she tumbled him over and over, up-setting his thoughts and plans and decisions, turning him in directions he'd never intended to go.

"I'm going to kiss you now," he warned.

Her hands scaled his chest before wrapping around his neck. "Did I mention you kissed like a dream?"

"I seem to remember reading that somewhere." He brushed his mouth over hers. "I'll do my best not to disappoint you."

The instant their lips sealed, he didn't worry about disappointing her. All thought left him but one. To pos-sess what she so generously offered. To plunder her mouth with sweet savagery. Pure desire pounded through him and all he could think about was consuming her, bit by luscious bit. Her head tipped back and her mouth parted, giving him full access. He didn't waste any time, but stroked inward.

It wasn't enough. Not nearly enough. Ever since she'd first marched past him in her colorful cropped tops, he'd wanted to explore what lay beneath the flirty scrap of silk. He couldn't resist the temptation any longer, especially not after what he'd seen from his vantage point in the garden.

"Hang on, sweetheart," he warned.

Sliding his hands along the flat planes of her belly, he swept upward, filling his palms with the soft unfettered weight of her breasts. He groaned into her mouth. Heaven help him, but he'd died and gone to fly with the angels. Or maybe he'd descended into hell, since he couldn't possess what he was so thoroughly exploring. More than anything, he wanted to forget all his fine ideals—or what was left of them—and drop this woman to the floor and make her his in every way possible.

A soft cry slipped from her lips to his and she covered his hands with hers, encouraging his touch. He backed her against the closed door, thrusting his hips into the cradle of hers. He cupped her bottom and lifted. She didn't need any prompting, but wrapped her legs around his waist, clutching him tight. Taking her mouth in another demanding kiss, he shoved up her shirt, exposing her breasts. They were incredible, round and plump and tipped in the same hot pink as the bougainvillea blossoms tangled in her curls. He shaped her breasts, flicking his thumbs over the hardened peaks. And then he closed his teeth over them. Ever so gently he tugged.

The instant Sami's cry rose to a shriek, Loner howled in concert.

Noah froze, silently running through his entire vocabulary of curses. Slowly, he released Sami and straightened. Her breath came fast and furious, her desperate gaze locking with his.

"Does this mean we're not going to finish what we started?" she panted.

"Not unless we're willing to let the entire household know what we're up to."

"I could live with it, but I doubt you could." To his everlasting regret, she lowered her shirt. "So where do we go from here?"

"That depends on you." He fought to recover some semblance of control. "What's your decision? Do you want to see where this leads?"

She shivered. "I think we both know where this is heading."

"But there's time to go slow, isn't there?" Was he asking her or warning himself? He'd pushed things with that kiss. If he'd pushed any further, all his fine talk about establishing a relationship first would have been moot. "There's no rush, right?"

For some reason his questions prompted tears. "But I've waited so long."

"Will a little longer make that much of a difference?" He feathered a kiss along her neck as he waited for her response. "I seem to remember you asking me to have a physical before we got down to business."

Her laugh caught in her throat. "You don't mind?"

"I'm not thrilled at the idea." He drew back, a thought occurring to him, one that would offer him some peace of mind—at least on one front. "I know. How about a trade-off?"

"What sort of trade-off?" she asked warily, stepping away from the door.

"I go for my physical like a good boy and you let me teach you some self-defense maneuvers. After your run-in with Thomas, you could use them."

Her brows drew together in bewilderment. "Is that

necessary? It's not like I'm at risk or in any sort of danger. Not if I cancel the rest of my interviews.''

"Humor me. How about if I teach you, and Daria, Carmela and Widget, as well. We'll start today. It'll be fun," he coaxed. "It's the perfect addition to the skills you're already teaching them.''

"Today, huh?''

"Within the hour," he pressed. Any skills she picked up from him would help protect her from her black-mailer.

"Okay. One more favor, though.''

Uh-oh. "What?''

She nibbled on her lip in a way that warned he wouldn't like this particular "favor.'' "I might have mentioned that I have a birthday coming up?''

"I recall something to that affect.''

"Well, Babe's throwing this big bash and…'' She clasped her hands together. "I'd really, truly appreciate it if you'd escort me.''

That wasn't so bad. "Sure.''

"You'd have to wear a tux.'' She shot him a hesitant look. "I can provide you with one.''

"That's not necessary.''

She lifted an eyebrow. "My man Friday comes complete with evening wear?''

"Consider me a full-service man Friday.'' He sighed. "More full-service than I realized when I first took the job. But that's my fault, I suppose.''

She was kind enough to let the remark pass. "There's one more, teeny-weeny detail.''

Hell. "What?''

"You need to leave Loner behind.''

"Not a chance.''

"It's at the Hyatt Regency in Embarcadero. They won't allow Loner in. Besides, if he freaks any of the guests, they're likely to call in animal control. I have a sneaking suspicion the authorities will take one look at him and get the impression—the *mistaken* impression— that he's a wolf."

She was more accurate than she knew. Discretion seemed the best choice at this point. "I guess I can leave him behind for one night."

"Great." Not giving him time to reconsider, she darted toward the door, throwing a quick grin over her shoulder. "Fair's fair. Since you've agree to all of my demands, I'll round up everybody so you can give us our first self-defense lesson."

The minute she left, Noah closed his eyes and slumped against the nearest wall. What the hell had he done? And how the hell was he going to get out of it? Get out of it? His mouth curved into a humorless smile. He didn't want out. He wanted in. All the way in. Which created one small problem....

How did he convince Sami to open the door?

Sami curled up in her chair behind the desk in the practice interview room and checked Mr. Woof for more rips. There weren't any since she'd last repaired him, but that didn't stop her from looking.

She cradled the stuffed animal in her arms, her thoughts turning to Noah. Maybe she was making a mistake about this baby business. Maybe he had a valid point and she was rushing into it without due thought. Even as she considered his comments, a bone-deep yearning filled her.

It had been so long since she'd last been part of a

family and a silent desperation encircled her like a shroud. Perhaps the desire to have a baby had come to a head when her mother had moved out, leaving her to rattle around the house alone. Maybe it was because it was spring and spring brought back dark memories— memories she wanted to replace with some life-affirming act. Or maybe it had something to do with this particular birthday—a year she'd dreaded for two solid decades.

Was her desire to have a baby so wrong just because she couldn't put it in terms Noah would understand? Did it make her arms ache any less? No. Nor did it ease her fears about wedded bliss. Should she give up on her desire to have a baby just because she wasn't married, or because Noah's comments had pricked her conscience?

Marriage. A husband. Commitment. Loss.

It was all so confusing. An image of Noah slipping into her mind, an image of him gathering her close and covering her mouth with his kisses. Of Noah carrying her to his bed. Of him holding their baby in his arms. Of the years marching past with Noah at her side.

It was so terribly tempting. Clutching Mr. Woof closer, Sami bowed her head, helpless tears slipping down her cheeks.

What the hell was she going to do?

Noah waited at the bottom of the steps and checked his watch. They were running late. Despite Sami's rather unique, if less-than-fortunate, personality traits, he'd always found her punctual. He had to assume the delay was due to her reluctance to attend her birthday party, which didn't make a bit of sense. He frowned. Why would Babe insist on throwing such a huge bash when Sami was so opposed to the idea?

Unfortunately, it wasn't his place to say anything, at least not while playing the part of Sami's secret bodyguard. And especially not when he hadn't done a damn thing about uncovering her blackmailer. He hadn't heard back on the fingerprints, yet. But the background checks he'd run hadn't turned up any useful information. Worse, he was finding it more and more difficult to keep his mind on the job instead of on a certain sparkling blonde.

A small noise alerted him to her approach and he turned, watching in undisguised pleasure as Sami drifted down the steps toward the foyer. She wore her curls swept into an unusually formal style, piled on top of her head, though a few stubborn tendrils had already escaped. He couldn't help wondering how long it would take before the rest came tumbling down.

His gaze shifted to the chic red evening dress she wore. Except for the fact that it left one shoulder bare, it reminded him of a twenties flapper dress. She'd even found a matching beaded headband and decorated it with a huge peacock feather that bobbed with each bouncing step she took. As a final touch, a red-beaded wrap trailed in her wake. It suited her perfectly.

To his amusement, she'd actually worn high heels and he couldn't help wondering which would come undone first—her hair or those sexy red suede heels. Noah grinned. Of course, if he had his way it would be her snazzy little dress.

"Wow!" she said, greeting him with a wide smile. "You look incredible in that tux."

"Like it?"

"And it's black and everything," she marveled, joining him at the foot of the steps. "Imagine that."

"Hey, my shirt's white."

"So I noticed." She slowly circled him. "I can hardly believe it. What happened? Are all your black ones in the laundry?"

"I'll have you know, I wore this white shirt just for you," he claimed with mock indignation. "You seemed so concerned about my lack of color choices that I thought I'd reassure you that I do own something besides black."

She shook her head in disbelief. "From black to white. Will wonders never cease. I'm not sure I can handle the change."

"I have every confidence in your ability to deal with such a life-altering experience." He held out his hand. "Enough about me. You're gorgeous, sweetheart. Good enough to eat."

Sami linked her fingers with his and offered a mischievous grin that did odd things to his midsection. "As good as chocolate?"

"Better."

She wrinkled her nose at him. "Impossible. There's nothing better than chocolate."

He simply shot her a speaking look and waited. It didn't take long. Her mouth formed a pretty red "O" and a blush slipped along her cheekbones. Satisfied that she'd taken his meaning without him having said a word, he leaned down and kissed her, a thorough joining of their mouths that was long and deep and as satisfying as it was frustrating.

"As soon as I have my exam I'll prove it's better than

chocolate,'' he murmured, sliding his thumb across her lower lip.

Her eyes acquired a dazed expression that left him secretly amused. The flapper had come unflapped. ''I believe you,'' she said. ''I didn't think it was possible, but I may have to rethink that position.''

Her peacock feather trailed drunkenly down her back and he carefully adjusted it beneath her headband. ''There. Perfect. Are you ready?''

Instantly, her passionate glow dimmed. ''Not really. I suppose it would be bad form to play hooky from my own birthday party?''

'''Fraid so.''

She slanted him a suggestive glance. ''I can think of something else we could do instead.''

''So can I.'' He regarded her steadily. ''But I refuse to play second choice to your birthday party.''

''Actually, you'd be first choice.''

''Thank you. But it's not going to happen.''

She snapped her fingers and turned back toward the steps, darting up the first couple. ''You know, I think I forgot my lipstick. Wait right there and I'll—''

Her comment ended in a shriek as Noah swung her off the steps and into his arms. ''Come along, Cinderella. Your ball awaits.''

''But my lipstick,'' she protested.

''Don't bother. I'll just kiss it off again.''

''In that case…'' She wrapped her arms around his neck. ''Carry on, Prince Charming. Off to our pumpkin carriage.''

Their pumpkin carriage turned out to be the limo Reggie had put at their disposal. His driver, Bill, proved to be every bit as impressively large as Pudge had claimed. He grinned as Noah emerged from the house carrying Sami. Tipping his cap, he opened the limo door. "Good evening, sir. Ma'am."

"Hi, Bill. How's it going?"

"Just fine, Ms. Sami. Happy Birthday."

She scowled. "You don't need to remind me."

He nodded sympathetically. "Number twenty-nine is always a tough one."

That perked her right up. "Yes, it is. And it will be again next year."

He winked. "I'll keep that in mind."

The drive to the Hyatt Regency didn't take long. Sami loved the hotel, which was no doubt why her mother had chosen it. From the distinctive glass elevators and cascading foliage, to the center fountain and the four-piece orchestra playing classical music, she often came here to sit and talk with a friend over a glass of wine. Under any other circumstances, she'd have been delighted for an excuse to visit. But not today.

"You're eating off the last of your lipstick," Noah warned.

"Am I? Sorry. Nerves."

"I would have thought a party was right up your alley."

"I guess you don't know me as well as you thought."

He'd gone silent again and she shot him a quick glance. Darn it all. Those silences of his annoyed her. They had the uncanny result of making her think. And tonight thinking was the last thing she wanted to do.

"Okay, you do know me well," she said.

"So if it's not the party, it must be your birthday."

"Yes."

He slipped an arm around her waist and pulled her

close, drawing her to a halt. "I never thought I'd have to twist your arm to get you to talk. You've always been straightforward with me."

Her temper flared. "Is that a criticism?"

"It's an observation," he said evenly. "Something's wrong. Is it celebrating another birthday?"

"No! Yes. Not really."

He nodded sagely. "Got it."

"Darn it, Noah. Birthdays are always hard for me."

"Why?"

To her dismay, tears pricked her eyes. "I can't discuss it. Not now. I'll never be able to get through the evening if I explain."

"Then we won't discuss it." He'd pulled a snowy white handkerchief from his pocket. Tipping up her chin, he dabbed at her eyes. "It'll work out. You'll see."

"Noah…"

He stopped her words with his fingertip. "You look beautiful." He smiled with such tenderness it stole her breath. "But then, you always look beautiful."

"Even in multicolored toenail polish, with my hair going every which way and no makeup?"

"Especially then. Gum-smacking, bracelets clattering, barefoot and cocky, flowers or even feathers stuck in her hair." His voice had deepened, his gray eyes alight with an emotion she didn't dare name. "That's the Sami we all know and love."

# CHAPTER EIGHT

OH, NO. Sami fought to breathe. Noah had used the "L" word. It was her birthday, the worst day of each year, and he'd used the "L" word. Could it get any worse? She had to find a way out of this. "We're going to be late."

"We're already late," he said with a shrug.

She attempted a smile. It was shaky, but at least her mouth curved in the appropriate direction. "You may have noticed that I'm usually good at coming up with excuses off the top of my head. I guess it goes with having a 'barefoot and cocky' type of personality. But to be honest—" Her chin quivered despite her best attempts to control it. She didn't doubt for a moment that Noah caught the telltale movement. "I need to find a way of getting myself out of this conversation. So, do you think you could just go along with the 'we're late' excuse?"

"Sorry. I didn't mean to push." He stepped closer and adjusted first the feather in her headband and then her fringed shawl, his touch a gentle balm. "Don't worry. No one will realize anything's wrong."

He'd read her mind and with a simple sentence, eased her fears. No one would know she was upset, that her bubbly smile lacked sincerity or that the dampness in her eyes didn't come from excitement. She swallowed hard. "Thanks."

"Anytime."

He offered his elbow and she slipped her hand into the crook of his arm. She could feel the delicious play of muscles and tendons beneath her fingertips, even through the thickness of his jacket. Amazing. With his dark, wavy hair and calm silver eyes, Noah looked as incredible in a tux as he did in jeans and a T-shirt.

Where on earth had her mother found him? His type was in short supply in the world she inhabited. He was a fiercely protective man, adept at taking charge at a moment's notice, as well as a man who inspired confidence and loyalty. Moreover, he was someone who understood a woman's deepest fears and did his best to allay them.

It puzzled her. He could be anyone, do anything. Why had he chosen to play man Friday to her crazy household when he was capable of so much more? She shot him a quick look. Perhaps this would be a good time to ask. In fact, she didn't understand why she hadn't thought to question him sooner. Maybe if she hadn't been so obsessed with finding a father for her baby, she would have.

"Noah—"

He glanced down at her. "I don't suppose anyone would be too upset if you slipped away once the cake has been cut and the presents opened. Knowing Babe's generosity, the champagne will be flowing. In another hour or so, it'll be a wonder if your guests even remember what they're celebrating." He slanted her an infectious grin. "What do you say? Do you want to sneak off when nobody's watching? Would that make you feel better?"

All thoughts but one scattered into the night. "I'm afraid Babe's going to announce her next engagement."

Sami had no idea where the words came from, but once spoken she realized they expressed another worry that had been gnawing at her all day.

"Is that why—"

"No," she interrupted hastily. "I was wondering what other disaster could happen and that popped into my head."

For some reason her comment elicited a dark frown. "Do you have a bad feeling about tonight?"

"Good grief, Noah. Haven't you been listening?" Her voice carried an edginess that alarmed her. But she couldn't seem to control it. "I've been telling you that ever since we got here."

He didn't react to her tone, which only made her feel worse. "I want you to do me a favor," he said.

"What?"

"Stay close tonight."

Her brows drew together in bewilderment. "Close? Why?"

"Do it in exchange for the favor I'm doing you."

"What favor is that?"

"See if any of this rings a bell." He held up his thumb. "First you talked me into escorting you to this little shindig, not to mention wearing a monkey suit." He flicked his index finger upward. "And second, you convinced me to leave Loner at home. He usually provides an extra set of eyes and ears. Not to mention a better than average nose. I'm at a disadvantage without him."

A smile slipped across her mouth, the first truly natural one since they'd arrived at the hotel. "Were you planning to track me down?"

"Only if you disappear on me." He'd turned serious

and it alarmed her. "Promise me, Sami. Promise you'll stay close tonight."

"Fine. I promise."

"Good." He inclined his head toward the room they were approaching. "Show time, sweetheart. I just caught a glimpse of your mother, so smile. If Babe senses something's wrong, she'll never let up."

"You really do know my mother." It reminded her of the questions that had plagued her earlier. "You said she hired you. But you never said how you met."

"Didn't I?"

There wasn't time to ask anything further, but Sami made a mental note to pursue the conversation at the first opportunity. The instant they stepped into the ballroom, Babe descended on them, dispensing hugs and kisses and chattering away at high speed. She only drew breath long enough to shoot Noah a quick look. It held an unmistakable question, expressing both nervousness and—

Sami's eyes widened in dawning disbelief. And guilt. A nasty little thought flittered through her mind, leaving behind a terrible suspicion. Her hands clenched around her wrap, her grip so hard the beaded decoration cut into her palms. *Oh, no. Please, not that.* It had never occurred to her that Babe might have a personal interest in Noah—that that might explain how they knew each other so well. But it was there in her mother's beseeching gaze as well as in Noah's answer—a silent, glittering warning that elicited instant obedience.

Sami hadn't thought the evening could get any worse. What an idiot she'd been. It had gone from disastrous directly to horrifying. Her mother and Noah. Heaven help her. What in the world should she do now?

"Hello, my dear." Reggie appeared at Sami's side and planted an avuncular kiss on her cheek. "I'd wish you a happy birthday, but I'd need your promise not to take my head off first."

She turned to her uncle in relief, a gurgle of laughter covering the advent of tears. "You can keep your head."

"Why, thank you." He handed her a glass of champagne and lifted an eyebrow in question. "You strike me as a woman who could use this. Or am I mistaken?"

"No, you're right. I could."

"I was hoping we might find a few minutes to talk privately. But looking at you, I suspect my timing's off again."

"You know I always have time for you, Uncle Reg." She linked arms with him. "Come on. Let's find a quiet corner and—"

He shook his head. "Not now, I don't think." Gesturing to indicate the decorations, he deliberately changed the subject. "So? Do you like how your mother's fixed up the place?"

Sami took a quick sip of champagne and scanned the room. Flowers, tulle and silver foil made up a predominate portion of the decor. "As always, Babe's pulled it off in style."

"She's done a beautiful job, though it looks more like a wedding reception than a birthday party." He gave an abashed shrug. "But maybe that's because I'm a man and don't have an eye for these things."

"Or maybe you're right and it looks that way because she's had more practice at weddings than birthdays."

Reggie inhaled sharply and turned, staring at her in astonishment. "What did you say?"

"I…I said…" To Sami's horror, tears filled her eyes. "I said something really rude and horrible, didn't I?"

"Yes, my dear. You did. I believe the question is… Why?"

She darted a stricken look toward Noah. As though sensing her desperation, his gaze shifted and he focused on her. Their communication was instantaneous, a silent exchange of thought and emotion, a desperate plea sent winging out and an immediate reassurance sent swiftly back. Murmuring an excuse to Babe, he crossed to her side.

"I believe they're playing our song," he said, nodding toward Reggie. Taking the champagne flute from Sami, he handed it to a passing waiter. "Excuse us, won't you?"

With a smoothness she could only envy, he wrapped his arms around her and swung her onto the floor. "What's going on?" he bit out. "What did Reggie say to you?"

*"Nothing."*

"Don't give me that. You were about to burst into tears. Now what the hell happened?"

She couldn't look at him, couldn't bear to see his expression when she explained. "He said the place appeared more like a wedding reception than a birthday party."

Noah's brows drew together as he attempted to attach meaning to her comment. "And that made you cry?"

"No. It was what I said in reply." She moistened her lips, forcing out the confession. "I…I told him that was because Babe's had more practice at wedding receptions."

He dismissed her comment out of hand. "Bull. You'd never say anything that cutting."

"But I did." She sniffed, her tears returning with a vengeance. "I really did."

He swung her deeper into the room, giving her time to recover before asking his next question. "What prompted it?"

The truth came tumbling out. "She looked at you."

He missed his footing. "Come again?"

"My mother looked at you." She thumped his chest with her fist. "And darn it, Noah. You looked back."

"Okay. That's about as clear as mud."

"Maybe this will clarify matters for you." She forced herself to meet his gaze, to see his reaction when she asked her question. "Are you having an affair with Babe?"

"Have you lost your mind?" he asked, icily polite.

"Please say no. Please tell me you're not—" She couldn't say it. It hurt too much.

He pulled her close, so close she could hear the reassuring beat of his heart. It echoed in her ears, steady and comforting. "No. I'm not having an affair with your mother." To her profound relief, not a hint of laughter disturbed the even tenor of his voice. "No, I don't ever plan to have one with her. And no, I have never had any romantic connection with her in the past. There. Does that satisfy you?"

She nestled into the crook of his shoulder and drew a shaky breath. "I'm sorry. I don't know what got into me. I saw her give you this odd look and then you gave her one and then—"

His smile disturbed the curls above her headband. "And then your imagination took over?"

"Something like that," she confessed gruffly. "It's just that I don't know how you two met. Or why she chose you for my birthday present. Or what you're doing in my house. Come to think of it, nothing about you makes much sense."

"Sure it does."

His hand forged a leisurely path the length of her spine, chasing away every thought except a single, dangerously illicit one. She wanted to make babies with this man. Many, many plump, happy, silver-eyed babies. She cleared her throat and struggled to focus. "Refresh my memory. You were saying?"

He grinned knowingly. "I was saying that your mother's decision makes sense." Was that what she'd asked? She couldn't remember anymore. "Babe chose me for your present because I'm trustworthy and because she knew that I could protect you. See? It makes complete sense."

Sami snorted. "Yeah, right. Like I need protection. The only one I need protection from is you."

He muttered something beneath his breath, something that didn't bear repeating. "I suspect Babe would agree with that."

"Which explains the look you two exchanged," Sami guessed. "I suppose Mother was worried that something had happened between us."

"She wouldn't be wrong, would she?"

"No." Sami caught her bottom lip between her teeth. "Funny. I'd have thought she'd be pleased. She's always introducing me to 'perfect' men. I finally find one I think fits that description and she's opposed to it." She peeked up at him. "She *is* opposed to it, right? You're sure about that?"

"Positive. I believe she feels we're too different. She called us night and day." He swung Sami in a tight circle, locking her hips against his, their steps in total accord. "She's not wrong, is she?"

"No," Sami whispered. "She's not wrong."

"And it doesn't matter that you think I'm perfect, does it? You're not in the market for permanent."

Her laugh was ripe with pain. "That's why we're opposites. You want one thing and I'm after—"

"The opposite."

"Right."

They continued to dance in silence, which was reasonable, Sami decided. They'd said it all, hadn't they? They *were* as different as night and day. She shied away from commitment while he welcomed it. He kept a tight lid on his emotions, while she leaked them all over everyone and everything. He was the most perfect man she'd ever met and she... Her mouth trembled. She was a total idiot to shy away from something she wanted so badly.

No sooner did the music fade into silence when Babe joined them. She slipped in between, separating them, and wrapped her arm around Sami's waist. "I thought we'd get the festivities started early, if you two are finished with each other." She flashed a quick smile in Noah's direction. "Otherwise, my darling daughter will disappear the first time I turn my back."

Sami winced. "I'd have waited a little longer than the first time you turned your back," she lied.

"Like the second?" Babe's laughter rang out. "Come on. You can't fool me. Let's get the cake cut. If you thank our guests for their presents at the same time, you can have everything over with at once."

"Presents? Oh, Mom. You didn't have people bring gifts, did you?"

"You know me better than that. I requested everyone make donations to the local woman's shelter in your name." She tugged on Sami's arm. "Let's go."

Sami resisted, her gaze locking with Noah's. "Aren't you coming?"

He shook his head. "I can watch from here."

"You said you'd stick close," she persisted doggedly.

His mouth twisted. "I'm as close as I'm likely to get." The words hit and hit hard. "I'm your man Friday, remember? It would be better if we both keep that in mind."

The music started up again and couples began drifting across the floor, slipping into the space separating her from Noah, parting them further still. The distance between them grew. She'd have gone to him, but Babe pulled her away.

"Hurry," she urged. "They're bringing out the cake."

Sami forced a cheerful smile to her lips, but something had broken inside. She didn't understand it. She wasn't a woman capable of loving a man. She didn't want to fall in love. Love meant loss. Love ended. Love hurt. But she'd have given anything in that moment to have Noah's strong arms around her, his husky voice rumbling in her ear, his gray eyes fixed on hers, filled with quiet understanding.

All around people were singing and cheering. She searched the room, desperate to catch a glimpse of Noah. But he'd disappeared from view.

"Time to blow out the candles," someone shouted.

More voices called out. "How many this year?"

"Twenty-nine."

"*Again?*"

"You can do it, Sami. Make a wish," Babe prompted.

"Better make a wish that you get to be twenty-nine again next year," a woman from the crowd suggested.

"Oh, no," Babe shot back. "She's better off wishing we believed it!"

Good-natured laughter rippled all around and even Sami joined in. These were her friends and they meant well. They couldn't know how difficult this night was for her. Babe presented a cake knife with a flourish and Sami spent time cutting slices and exchanging gossip with the guests. For those few, precious moments the shadows were held at bay and her laughter came easily. She even relaxed enough to enjoy herself.

After thanking her guests for their contributions to the woman's shelter, she flitted from group to group, doing her best to make everyone feel welcome. Noah had been right. The champagne flowed freely and by the time she'd circled the room, no one even remembered it was her birthday.

Thank goodness for small favors.

Babe approached, Reggie on her arm. "See? That wasn't so bad," she said with a tentative smile. "I don't know why you were in such a panic over a little ol' birthday."

"Damn it, Babe." Reggie glared in a rare display of anger. "You know why birthdays are difficult for her."

Pain shadowed Babe's expression. "Of course I know."

"I support most of your decisions, my dear." He shook his head. "But this wasn't one of your best."

"Oh, Mother. It's not all my birthdays that are so

tough to take,'' Sami whispered. ''It's *this* birthday. If you'd thrown a party last year or even when I turned thirty-two, it wouldn't have been so bad. But did it have to be this year?''

''Don't you understand? That's why I did it. It's time to move on.'' Tears burned in Babe's eyes. ''You can't keep living in the past, Sami. You need to embrace life, not hide from it. I know you don't believe me, but you deserve to celebrate. And you deserve it this year most of all.''

Sami didn't wait to hear more. Spinning away, she thrust through the crowd. People called to her, but she simply gave a shaky smile and a wave and pushed on. If it weren't for her heels, she'd have made better progress and swearing beneath her breath, she fought to release the minuscule straps. Kicking them off, she hurried toward the exit. Finally, *finally*, she was out the door, racing through the lobby of the Hyatt.

With luck, Reggie's limo would still be available. If she could just make it to the street. If she could just hold out for another minute or two. A sob ripped loose. And then another. To her relief, she caught a glimpse of the limo right outside the door. Bill, bless his heart, had commandeered the space in a No Parking zone. The instant she erupted from the hotel, he opened the back door.

She flung herself inside. No sooner had the door slammed behind her than the tears came, fast and noisy and turbulent. Hot tears, messy tears, two decades' worth of agony rising up from the depths of her soul and spilling down her cheeks.

*Where was Noah?* Where was he when she needed him most? And then she remembered.

They were night and day. Opposites destined to meet, but never unite.

Noah didn't have to see Sami leave to know she'd gone. It was as though the life and energy had been abruptly snuffed from the party. He started for the exit, his suspicions confirmed when he found a familiar-looking pair of red suede shoes carelessly discarded near the door. Snatching them up, he went after her, calling himself every sort of idiot.

He'd been hired to protect Sami, to find out who was blackmailing her. Instead, he'd raised as many barriers between them as possible...before deserting her. He could only hope she wouldn't be forced to pay the ultimate price for his stupidity. Just imagining the potential consequences had him breaking into a trot.

Next, he came across her peacock feather lying forlornly near the fountain and snagged that, as well. Racing down the escalator, he slammed through the doors onto the street outside the Hyatt, arriving just in time to see Reggie's limo pull away. He swore furiously. This was all his fault. He should have stuck by her side like he'd promised. Lifting his arm, he whistled for a cab. At least he knew she hadn't been snatched, though he found it poor consolation.

The fact remained that she could have been taken and he wouldn't have been anywhere around to prevent it from happening.

The drive to Pacific Heights seemed interminable. The second the cab drew to a halt, Noah tossed a twenty at the driver and bolted for the front door. Darkness enshrouded the hallway, the silence oppressive rather than comforting. Who'd have thought he'd long for the day when bracelets chattered and bare feet slapped against red oak flooring while a miniature blond dynamo scolded Loner for playing with her toys?

At the thought of his constant shadow, Noah called softly, relieved when the animal padded obediently into the foyer. If anything had happened to Sami, the dog would have lost no time in communicating that fact. "Find her," Noah ordered, signaling his instructions.

Loner took off down the hallway and dashed up the steps to the second story. Noah followed, startled to discover the dog sitting at attention outside of his bedroom door.

"She's in there?" He gave Loner's ears an appreciative scratch. "Stay here, boy. Guard the door. I don't want anyone disturbing us."

Leaving the dog at his post, Noah quietly entered the room. None of the lights had been turned on, but he didn't need them. He knew where he'd find her. Silently crossing to the windows, he stood in front of the semi-transparent drapes. Sami was curled up in the bench seat on the far side, staring out at the scattered lights dotting the blackened bay. Looking for sea monsters or making wishes?

He searched for the right words to open the conversation. But all he came up with was a rather lame line. "You left the party without me, Cinderella."

"I'm sorry." She'd been crying, he could hear it in her voice. As always, it tied him into knots, left him helpless to know how to fix the problem. "That was rude of me."

"You don't need to apologize." He swept the curtain to one side and set her shoes next to her. "You also forgot these."

Still she didn't look at him. "I do that a lot, don't I?"

"I've noticed a certain tendency on your part to lose shoes." He cupped her shoulders and massaged the tension kinking her muscles. "What's wrong, Sami? Why did you run off?"

She shrugged. "I needed to bring a fast end to a bad night."

"I assume something brought the evening to a head." He waited a beat. "Would you like to tell me about it?"

"Not really." Her shoulders grew rigid beneath his hands. "But I will, anyway. You deserve an explanation after all you've done for me."

"Explain because you want to, not because you think I deserve to know." When she didn't say anything further, he prompted, "Why is your birthday such a difficult time for you?" He took a wild guess. "Is it the day your father died?"

"No. No, not that." He heard the harsh give and take of her breath. "It's the day my sister was born."

"You have a sister?" he asked in astonishment. "A twin?"

She shook her head. "We were born on the same day, but ten years apart."

"I don't understand."

"It's simple. Nancy would have been twenty-one today. A fully matured adult." Sami's voice dropped. "At least, she would have been if she'd lived."

He began to comprehend. "Aw, hell, Sami. I'm so sorry."

"She was killed in the same accident as my father."

"I can understand why that would make your birthday tough, but—"

"It isn't because she died," Sami corrected sharply.

"If it's not that, what is it?"

Her voice dropped to a whisper. "It's the way she died. That's why my birthday is sometimes tough to take. Why this one, in particular, is nearly impossible for me to deal with." Sami's hands collapsed into fists, the knuckles deathly white in the darkened room. "It's not fair! She should have lived to become an adult. That party tonight should have been for her, not for me. But she didn't live and we didn't get to toast her coming of age. And it's all because of me. I killed her, Noah. It's my fault she died!"

# CHAPTER NINE

Noah swore softly. "I thought you said she was killed with your father. That it was a car accident."

Sami tucked into a tighter ball, resting her chin on her bent knees, her dress a faint glow of red in the darkened room. "Nancy was such a sweet thing," she commented. "Have I told you that already?"

Noah schooled himself to patience, aware she needed to explain what happened in her own way, in her own time. "No, you haven't."

"I absolutely adored her. Anything she wanted, I gave her." Ever so gently she set Mr. Woof on the seat beside her. "This was the first birthday present I ever bought her. And the last."

Understanding dawned. "That's why you panicked when you saw Loner with it."

"It was Nancy's favorite toy. She took it everywhere. It's the one memento I have of her."

He had to get Sami to tell her story, to lance the wound that had festered for so many years. "Why do you blame yourself for Nancy's death?"

"Because it *was* my fault." A hint of anger rippled through her voice, but he let it go. At least it was an honest emotion instead of the surreal calm that had gripped her earlier.

"Tell me more."

Slowly, she removed her headband and tossed it aside,

taking a moment to massage her temples before speaking again. "We were stopped at a red light."

"*We?*"

"Didn't I mention?" Her laugh was barren of humor. "I was in the car, too."

He fought to control his breathing, to keep from betraying his shock. "No. You didn't mention that before."

"Nancy had dropped Mr. Woof and I—" Her voice broke. "We were stopped. I thought it was safe."

He sat down beside her, drawing her into his arms. "Finish it, Sami. What did you do?"

"I was in the front seat next to Dad. Nancy was in the back. She'd dropped Mr. Woof and he'd rolled onto the floor of the car where I couldn't reach. But I could reach Nancy. So I unfastened her seatbelt and told her to get the toy. I thought she'd be okay. I swear I did." She curled into him, wrapping her arms around his waist, her breath shallow and rapid. "But then the light turned green. We started into the intersection. 'Hurry,' I said and... I remember my father's shout. He swore. Isn't that funny? He never swore. I remember the hideous shriek of metal. And I remember the pain before everything went dark."

"Another car hit you?"

She nodded. "It ran the red light and broadsided us. When I woke up I was in the hospital. Babe was there." Tears slipped down her cheeks. "But Nancy and Dad were gone."

"It wasn't your fault. You have to know that, right?" He gripped her shoulders. "You were eleven years old. It was a freak accident. You couldn't possibly have realized what might happen."

"Babe's told me the same thing. And most days I even believe it. But this birthday…" She shook her head. "It just hit hard. I feel guilty celebrating what would have been a special day for her."

"Tell me something, Sami. This baby business. How much of it has to do with your sister? Are you sure you're not trying to close a circle or replace her in some subconscious way?"

"Of course there's some of that," she conceded. "I'd be foolish to deny it. But it's not just Nancy. I adore children. I always have. The only reason I don't already have a half dozen is because I'm not married."

"So when did you decide that a husband was no longer a necessary component?"

"Recently." She pulled back, her expression settling into defensive lines. "There are lots of women raising children without benefit of husbands."

"And a lot of them wish they didn't have to. Wouldn't you have wanted your father in your life for longer than you had him?"

"That's not fair, Noah!"

He forced himself to ignore the rawness in her voice. He had to make her understand, to see how the choices she made in the coming months would affect the rest of her life—the rest of both their lives. "I'm not trying to make you feel worse, sweetheart. But don't you get it? You're still looking at this situation through the eyes of an eleven-year-old."

"I'm thirty-one, not eleven."

"Listen to me, Sami. You're a smart woman. Unfortunately, at an impressionable age, you watched your mother lose the man she adored. And then you watched as she flung herself from marriage to marriage trying to recapture what she'd shared with your father. No wonder you're terrified of making that sort of commitment.''

She shook her head. "Even if I found a man I could love, there aren't any guarantees. I'm as likely to lose him through divorce as death.''

"You're right. Life doesn't come with guarantees.'' He released his breath in a long sigh. "Look, I understand that you're afraid. You're afraid of opening your heart and giving all the love trapped inside. You're sure the person you choose to love will either die or leave you.''

"*Yes!*'' She pushed him away and escaped the window seat. "There. Are you satisfied now? I'm afraid. It's safer to stay single and avoid all that.''

"Do you think Babe would have avoided falling in love with your father if she'd had the choice? Do you think if she'd known in advance what would happen, she'd have refused to marry him?''

"I haven't a clue.''

"Yes, you do. I don't know Babe as well as you, and yet I can say without any hesitation that she'd have gone through with the marriage, no matter what the cost in the end.''

"You can't be certain of that.''

"Yes, I can. Damn it, Sami. Why the hell do you think she's married so many times?'' He didn't wait for an answer. "It's because she's still looking. She wants love in her life again. Sure, she's made mistakes. But she must think they're worth it if it means finding the sort of love she had with your father.''

Sami's mouth set in a stubborn line. "That's fine for Babe. I've made a different choice.''

"One that's based on fear." He stopped her before she could interrupt. "It isn't love you're afraid of. It's loss. Think about it, Sami. Let's say you go ahead with your plan to have a baby. Will you handle the loss of that child any better than you'd handle the loss of a husband?"

She stared at him, stricken.

"Don't you see? It wasn't just your father who died in that accident. Nancy died, too. I think you're having this baby so you can move forward with your life. To pick up, emotionally, where you left off all those years ago. But you'll never be able to do that until you face your fear and let go of it. You have to allow yourself to love without limits or conditions. Otherwise, fear will always keep you emotionally stunted."

"You're wrong!"

"Am I? What happens when that baby turns one?" he demanded. "Will you panic every time you're in the car with her? And what if she survives until she's two? You'll think, 'Phew, she lived longer than Nancy.' But then your imagination will come up with a whole new scenario, a whole new set of fears and worries and dangers that could hurt your child. You'll go from one fear to the next to the next. And you'll instill those fears in your child. You won't mean to, but it'll happen. That's what fear does to you. Don't you see? You don't really want a baby."

"How can you say that?"

"Because I've watched you. I've listened to you. I know what's in your heart. Whether you're willing to admit it or not, you want a complete family. One that will replace what you lost. That's why you were looking for the perfect father for your baby. Because he'll also be the perfect husband for you." He gathered her in his arms, searching for the words to convince her. "You're sweet and generous and kind. You open your home to strangers, trying to help them in every way you can. You're the most loving person I've ever met and yet when it comes knocking on your door, you push it away with both hands."

"No, I don't. And I can prove it to you." She encircled his neck with her arms. "Make love to me, Noah. Right now."

He shut his eyes, agonizing over the choice before him. "Why do you want me, Sami? It isn't like we've received the all-clear from the doctor."

"I don't care what the doctor has to say!"

"Maybe you want to practice for the main event. Is that it?" Wordlessly, she shook her head. His voice dropped, coaxing the truth from her. "Then is it because you're afraid? Any port in the storm?"

"No, no and no." Frustration edged her voice, but he refused to make it easy for her.

Releasing her, he stepped back and folded his arms across his chest. "Tell me why and make it the truth." He forced himself to wait her out, fighting the overriding urge to sweep her off her feet and carry her to his bed.

"Noah, please!" Her throat worked with painful desperation and it took three tries before she found the right words. "It's because we're incomplete on our own. Because together we're whole."

It was as close to a commitment as he was likely to get. He'd thrown some hard punches tonight and she'd taken them without flinching. She hadn't ordered him out or refused to listen. She hadn't liked what he'd said, but she'd stuck by him. That meant something. It had to.

"If I were smart, I'd kiss you goodnight and keep my hands to myself." His mouth curved in a self-mocking smile. "If I were really smart, I'd get the hell out of here now. Before it's too late."

"I hope to heavens that means you're not going to be smart." Her eyes were as luminous as the lights dotting the bay. "Otherwise, you'll force me to take drastic action."

That caught his attention. "What sort of drastic action?"

"I'd have to seduce you."

His smile grew. "And how would you go about that?"

She tilted her head to one side as she considered. "First I'd kiss you. The kind of kiss you'd exchange listening to Barry White's music. Ones that are slow and deep and vibrate all the way to your toes. Midnight kisses." A slumbrous quality entered her voice. "Bedroom kisses."

He nodded, conceding the point. "That might keep me standing here for a bit longer."

She drifted toward him, her dress whispering silken promises. "Then while you were standing there and I was kissing you senseless, I'd slip off your jacket and unbutton your shirt."

"Do you think taking off my shirt's enough to keep me from leaving?"

"There's no question in my mind."

He shot her a challenging look. "Prove it. First the kiss. Slow, deep and vibrating to my toes. That's what you promised in order to keep me here."

"And that's what you'll get."

Standing on tiptoe, she slid her fingers into his hair and captured his mouth with hers. Tilting her head to one side she gave him a thorough introduction to slow, followed by one in deep. Just when he thought she'd given him her best shot, she tugged at his bottom lip and proceeded to prove she knew precisely how to make him vibrate straight down to his toes.

Noah cupped her hips and aligned them with his, moving her against him to the music his imagination provided. "Remind me to play Barry White on a regular basis."

"Oh, but it gets better." Was she warning or promising? "Now midnight kisses."

She threatened his sanity with each lazy sweep of her tongue. Tantalizing him one minute, consuming him the next. Teasing with tiny nips before softening the kiss with the gentlest of caresses. Taking him with delicate parries, then aggressive demand.

He fought for breath. "If those are midnight kisses, what the hell qualifies as bedroom ones?"

Her lips slid to his earlobe and she whispered in wicked detail the difference between the two. His arousal was as instantaneous as it was painful. "Now do you understand why they're limited to the bedroom?" she teased.

"Because we'd be arrested if we tried it in public?"

"Well… One of us would." She wrapped her hands around his lapel and smiled up at him, her expression filled with an irresistible combination of mischief and hunger. "I believe I was supposed to be stripping you while kissing you senseless."

"Only if you're still intent on convincing me to stay."

"Trust me. I am."

Noah watched in wry amusement as she pushed and prodded his arms out of his jacket, finally discarding the Armani as though it were a used rag. It went winging through the air to crumple in a heap by the bed, his cummerbund following behind. Next shirt studs rained onto the floor like fallen stars and after what felt like an interminable delay she dragged his dress shirt off his shoulders. She'd bared him to the waist and he waited to see what she'd do next. She didn't leave him guessing for long.

With the lightest of touches, she trailed her fingertips across his shoulders to the hollow at the base of his throat, leaving behind a path of fire. "Do you want to go now?" she murmured.

He fought to organize his thoughts enough to speak. "I'm considering my options."

"Then I suggest you take this into consideration...."

Her index finger drifted down the center line of his chest, over the planes of his abdomen to the top of his trousers. He swallowed a groan. How did she manage to rouse such a reaction with one tiny finger? It didn't seem possible. She fixed her gaze on him, her rich green eyes filled with sultry promise. The opening of his trousers loosened and she flattened her hand against his belly, warming him with her heat.

"Have I convinced you to stay?"

"Almost." The word was torn from his throat, heavy and guttural and filled with demand.

"Almost?" Her rich laughter stirred an even more painful reaction. "You can't fool me, Noah. You're definitely going to stay. Shall I prove it to you?"

She didn't wait for an answer, but slipped beneath his

clothing, cupping his weight in her hands. She offered a smile as knowing as it was filled with ancient feminine mystique. And then, ever so gently, she squeezed.

A roaring filled his head and a cry welled up from someplace raw and elemental. He'd always prided himself on his control, always been the one to take charge. But that control was an illusion. Colors burst behind his closed eyelids. The same blazing orange and excruciating lime-green as the first outfit he'd seen her wear. Carnal Coral combined with Shell Shock Pink and Insatiable Indigo. They whirled through his mind like the colorful bracelets he seen whirling on a slender wrist.

Reason deserted him and he reached for her. The single shoulder strap of her flapper-style dress ripped beneath his hand. Silk rustled suggestively as it slipped from her body and pooled at her feet. She stood before him, unmoving, her skin touched with moonlight, her eyes filled with emerald fire, her moist lips the color of passion. Only the golden delta between her thighs remained shadowed, a scrap of black lace preserving her modesty.

Her breasts moved in a frantic rhythm with each give-and-take of her breath, signaling her arousal. It was his turn to reach out, to slide his index finger from the hollow of her throat to the tip of her breast. The rosy center puckered, a silent plea for his caress, and her groan echoed his, frantic and needy, a demand and an appeal all at the same time.

Slowly, she released him, the leisurely glide of her fingers an exquisite torture. "Does this mean you're staying?" she whispered.

His capacity for speech deserted him. He burned for this woman, his desire desperate and immediate, riding him harder than anything that had come before. Where was his ability to consider and analyze? With one touch this woman had pirated his reason, transforming him into something primitive and feral. His fist closed around the scrap of lace that concealed her from him.

"Take it off or I will," he warned.

Her smile took on a wild edge. "Do it."

The sound of rending cloth ripped away the last of his control. He tumbled her back onto the bed, shedding his trousers as he joined her. Tracing her body, he explored lush swells and soft indentation, drifting from sleek curves to moist hollows. Where once she'd promised to give him bedroom kisses, he bestowed them on her, edging her relentlessly toward a shattering completion.

She shuddered in his hold. "Please, Noah. I can't take any more." Tugging him into position, she locked her legs around him, encouraging his possession. "Now, Noah. Take me now."

He wanted to. He wanted to more than she could possibly know. But he couldn't. Not like this. "Not yet, Sami."

"Why?" she cried. "Noah, please."

"I can't." What bound them now was lust. And lust wasn't enough. Not anymore. "You have to say the words, sweetheart. Let me know this means more than satisfying a momentary urge. I can't give you casual. It's not in my nature."

Sami stared at Noah. Harsh color scored his cheekbones and his eyes were fixed on her, blazing with a dark desperation that could only be assuaged in one way. He wanted her, wanted her as frantically as she wanted him. But he held back, refusing to take her physically unless he had an emotional commitment, as well.

Everything he'd said to her, all that had taken place since he'd walked into her life solidified in that moment. The past blended with the present into a single pathway, while the future forked dramatically ahead. The first trail offered easy passage, smooth and rock-free, though there'd only be room for one traveler. She could traverse it untouched by pain, but girded by fear. The other could only be reached by throwing herself off a jagged cliff— one that had blocked her way for more years than she cared to count, one that forced a fall that would be long and hard and terrifying.

The only consolation was that Noah stood at the bottom of that cliff. Waiting. All she had to do was trust that he'd catch her. Trust. Commitment. Fear. Love. The words shrieked in her ears, battling within her soul.

"Noah!"

"I'm here, sweetheart. I have you."

She closed her eyes and wept. "I can't do it. I can't."

"It's okay to be afraid. It's not the fear that'll hurt you."

"It's the fall."

"It's not the fall. I promise that won't hurt you, either. It's walking away that will hurt. Don't walk away, Sami. Fight for what you want." He pushed a tumble of pale curls from her face. "Say the words, Sami. Take the risk."

"What happens if I won't?"

His forehead touched hers, his words feathering across her mouth. She could feel the tension build in him, feel him gather his impressive control. "It's all right, sweetheart. Nothing happens if you walk away. Nothing at all.''

Nothing, except he'd leave her alone in the bed, unfulfilled and hurting. *Take the risk!* Her eyelids fluttered open and she stared up at him. Taking a deep breath, she leaped. ''I love you, Noah. I love you more than life.''

She fell then, tumbling freely. The tears spilled down her cheeks, but this time Noah simply smiled. For a man who didn't ''do'' tears, he seemed to be handling them remarkably well.

''I love you, too, Sami,'' he said, gently wiping the dampness from her cheeks. ''You're everything I've ever looked for in a woman. You're everything I've ever wanted.''

He cupped her face, drugging her with the intoxicating kisses she'd described in such vivid detail a short time ago—long and slow and deep, vibrating all the way to her toes. But the craving she'd felt before was nothing compared to this. Perhaps it was the freedom that came from opening her heart. Or perhaps it came from her absolute trust in the man who held her secure in his arms.

Every tender sweep of his hand, every whispered endearment, every brush and scrape and caress was an expression of such intense rapture that she finally understood what her mother had lost all those years ago. The tears came again. Tears of regret that she'd almost missed experiencing such grace. That she'd tried to push something so wondrous from her life. That she'd have dared to believe that creating a child without such a bonding would have been acceptable.

Noah quieted her remorse with compassionate concern, his understanding absolute. "It's all right," he murmured. "Everything will be all right now."

"Make love to me, Noah. Show me how right it is," she pleaded.

He responded instantly, gathering her close. Each kiss drove her to a new plane of passion, each touch became a benediction, each whispered promise a commitment that bound them as one. Settling between her thighs, he joined with her so completely that she slipped beyond words, beyond rational thought, his lovemaking unlike anything she'd known before. He gifted her with life and she opened herself to him, giving Noah the one thing she'd never offered another man. The only thing she had available to offer.

She gave her love. All of it. Free and unconditionally, holding nothing back.

As they reached for the stars, the night fell heavily on them, blanketing them. And as they became sated and fulfilled, they grew still, curling into each other, a blissful tangle of arms and legs. And when they slept, it was a deep sleep, contented and serene.

For Sami, it was the most peaceful she'd known in two endless decades. Because at long last, she knew she'd found the family she'd lost all those years ago.

Noah awoke to an earsplitting scream. The moment he realized his arms were empty of anything small, feminine and delightfully passionate, he knew the worse had happened.

Sami had been taken.

It took every ounce of self-control not to panic. Exploding from the bed, he snatched up a pair of jeans, yanking them on in five seconds flat. Loner greeted him outside the door, barking hysterically. Together they ran, racing flat-out for the staircase leading to the foyer, taking the steps three at a time. Widget stood by the open front door. Spotting them, she screamed again. For someone who hadn't been able to speak above a whisper until now, she sure could raise hell when she chose.

"Where is she?" he demanded, skidding to a halt in front of her. "What happened to Sami?"

"He took her." Widget's breath came in half-hysterical pants. "A man took her."

With a shaking finger, she pointed to the bracelets scattered across the wooden floor and Noah closed his eyes. He'd know those colors anywhere. Insatiable Indigo. Carnal Coral. Shell Shock Pink. And a vivid red the exact color of the lipstick he'd kissed from Sami's mouth the night before. Loner sniffed the area, before collapsing on the floor, his nose inches from the bracelets. He released an odd-sounding whine, as though something about the odors confused him. Before Noah could ask any further questions, Pudge, Carmela and Daria came racing into the foyer. Rosie waddled behind at a more leisurely pace.

Noah gave Widget his full attention. "Tell me exactly what happened," he requested.

She nodded. "Okay. I'll do my best." She twisted her hands together like a nervous schoolgirl preparing to recite in front of a roomful of strangers. "First, the doorbell rang. Sami had just come down the stairs. I remember thinking that she was looking mighty pleased with herself—"

"Don't editorialize," Noah ground out. "Just get to the point."

Rosie chuckled. "Noah, you dirty dog. I knew if anyone could bring her around, you could.'' She looked at everyone in confusion. "So, what's up? Did I hear someone yell?''

Widget waved her silence. "This is serious, Rosie. Sami's been abducted.''

*"What!"*

Noah gripped Widget's shoulders and turned her to face him. "The only way I can help her is if you tell me precisely what happened. Sami came downstairs and the doorbell rang. I assume she opened it, right?''

Widget nodded. "Yes. There was a man standing there. He held out a box. Sami gave this happy shout. You know how she does? Anyway, the man picked her up, slung her over his shoulder and walked out.'' She began to cry. "Please, Noah. You have to do something. If it hadn't been for Sami I'd be rotting in jail, a menace to society.''

Aw, hell. Tears. Why did it have to be tears? "Take it easy,'' he soothed. "And try and concentrate. This man. Can you describe him?''

"He was big. Really big. A giant of a man.''

"Did he say anything? Did Sami?''

"He said, 'These are for you, Ms. Sami.' And she sort of squealed and...oh! She gave him a hug.''

Noah fought for breath. "She *hugged* him?''

"Well, I think that's because he gave her chocolates. You know how Sami is about chocolate.''

He swore beneath his breath. "Focus, Widget. The box contained *chocolates?* You're sure?''

"Positive. It was the same type she has all over the place. You know the ones I mean? The pretty gold foil boxes? Gosh, they're good. And she's so sweet about sharing them.''

He knew precisely the ones Widget meant. How many times had Sami pulled a box from some cubbyhole or drawer? *Chocolate makes everything better,* she'd said on more occasions than he could count. "Are you sure he abducted her?"

"Positive. After he handed her the box and she hugged him, he said, 'Sorry about this, Ms. Sami.' Then he picked her up and tossed her over his shoulder like she didn't weigh anything at all."

"What did Sami do?"

"She screamed." Widget caught her lip between her teeth. "But I think it was because she was surprised. Or maybe it was because her bracelets fell off."

"Did she fight him? Did she kick?" His voice rose despite his attempt to control it. "Did she do *anything* I've damn-it-to-hell taught the woman?"

Widget shifted from foot to foot. "She…er—"

*"What?"*

She winced. "Sami ripped the top off of the chocolates and ate one." She pointed to the corner of the foyer. "See? The lid's over there."

He turned to look. Sure enough, the lid lay discarded in the corner. He hadn't noticed it before. For some reason he had trouble drawing breath. "She ate the chocolates. That's it? She. Ate. The. *Chocolates?*"

"Just one." More tears flowed. "Then the guy tipped his cap in my direction and marched out the door and tossed her into his limo. That's all I remember."

Pudge tugged on Noah's arm, practically dancing with excitement. "A big guy with a limo. Get it?"

The two exchanged a glance of total accord. "Bill," they said at the same time.

Widget blinked in confusion. "That's right. How'd

you know?'' Her tears slowed. "I almost forgot that part. When he gave her the chocolates, she said, 'Thanks, Bill.'"

"Why in the world would Reggie's driver abduct Sami?" Rosie demanded.

Noah's mouth tightened. He didn't have an answer to that, but he knew what he intended to do about it. He thought of the odd-shaped "shaving kit" he'd hidden in his dresser drawer upstairs. Damn. Looked like it was time to break out his razor. "I don't know what Bill wants with her. Yet. But I'm going to find out."

"Oh, *Bill* wasn't abducting Sami." Noah and Rosie turned as one to stare at Widget. She smiled weakly. "I forgot that part, too. When he picked her up, he said, 'Sorry about this, Ms. Sami.'"

Noah thrust a hand through his hair, hanging on to his patience by a mere thread. "You mentioned that already."

"I know. But then he said, 'I have my instructions.' I'd guess that meant Bill was working for someone else." She glanced from one to the other. "Right?"

# CHAPTER TEN

"NOAH, this doesn't make a bit of sense," Babe insisted, nervously lighting her sixth cigarette since he'd arrived. "Why would Reggie abduct Sami? He adores that girl."

He didn't give a damn what Reggie's reasons were. The man was going down and Noah planned to make sure it hurt. At least now he understood what had bothered him about the blackmail notes. There hadn't been any contact information. No "Drop ten grand off at the third bench in Golden Gate Park." No phone number to call. Just the threat itself. Reggie had expected Sami to recognize who had sent the messages and respond accordingly.

Only, Sami had never received the notes.

Noah cursed himself for being such a fool. If he hadn't been so distracted by parts south of his belt buckle, he'd have caught on to that particular detail a hell of a lot sooner.

He paced the length of Babe's living room. In the past hour he'd discovered that it took precisely twenty strides to go from her phone to her picture window and a mere nineteen for the return trip. Useless information. Annoying information. Mind-numbing information that did absolutely nothing to cool his temper. "Have you gotten hold of him, yet?"

"No. And I've called the house and the limo number at least a hundred times. No one's answering."

"Where would he take her?" he rapped out. "Think, Babe."

"I have been thinking!" Lines of strain etched a path on either side of her mouth. She ground out her cigarette. "There's one possibility. Reggie has a small retreat in the mountains near Santa Cruz. It's isolated. A bit on the primitive side for my tastes, but—"

"Let's go."

"We don't know for sure that's where Reggie's taken her," she protested. "What if he calls while we're gone?"

"Then he'll discover no one's home. He'll either try again or he'll phone the house. Rosie has my cell number. She'll get hold of us." Noah cupped Babe's elbow, marching her out of her apartment and toward his Jeep where Loner anxiously waited. When she dug in her heels, he turned on her. "We're useless to Sami sitting here. Don't you get that? At least if we check the cabin we'll be doing something."

She capitulated without another word. Climbing behind the steering wheel, he headed south, picking up speed once they were clear of the city. Aside from Babe's occasionally offered directions, they accomplished the record-breaking ninety minute drive in tense silence. For the first time in her life, she seemed unwilling to indulge in casual chitchat, which came as an immense relief to Noah. When they were on the last leg of their journey, she finally broke the silence.

"The cabin's on the far side of this ridge," she said. "Turn left onto the dirt road around the next bend."

"Will he see us coming?"

"Yes. But only if you drive all the way to the end of

the road. The cabin's at the top and we'll be approaching from the back side. Right up until the final curve, we're concealed by trees. If you park at the base of the hill, we can hike up and chances are good we won't be spotted.''

He swung onto the dirt road, bouncing through ruts with careless disregard. ''There is no 'we,' Babe. You're waiting in the Jeep. Loner and I are taking care of this.''

''Not a chance,'' she protested. ''I'm not staying here by myself. I'll do something stupid if you leave me behind.''

''Better safe and stupid, then clever and injured.'' He nailed her with a grim look. ''At least I'll have managed to protect one of you.''

Babe sighed. ''Oh, Noah. You're not blaming yourself for Sami being taken, are you?''

''Of course I'm blaming myself,'' he retorted viciously. ''That's what happens when you let your guard down.''

Her expression gentled. ''Or when you allow someone to slip beneath your guard? It's personal between the two of you, isn't it?''

''If it wasn't, she'd be safe at home and I wouldn't be cursing myself for acting like an incompetent idiot.'' He swerved the Jeep to the side of the road and killed the engine. ''You might as well know right now. I'm in love with your daughter.''

Babe chuckled. ''Well, of course you are. You were supposed to fall in love with her.''

That caught him by surprise. ''I thought— You said we weren't right for each other.''

Her laughter grew, filling the Jeep. ''Honey, there

isn't a man alive who can stand being told no when it comes to a woman. If I'd thrown Sami at you, you'd have been out of there like a shot. But tell a man some pretty young thing is forbidden fruit and he can't keep his hands off her. I'm not above devious manipulation or relentless matchmaking. Why do you think I chose you in the first place?''

Aw, hell. ''You said it was because I owed you one.''

''There was no debt. You and I both know that, don't we?''

He was torn between amusement and irritation. ''We do now.''

''Don't be mad, sweetie. You meant well all those years ago. It's just that I'd already made up my mind not to marry Mel. But since you were intent on being noble and protective, I let you think you were saving me from disaster.'' She opened the Jeep door and shook her head in disgust. ''Men. You really do think blond means dumb.''

Blond did not mean dumb. Maybe he ought to write that down. He exited the Jeep, as well, surreptitiously signaling Loner to distract Babe. Under the cover of the dog's playful antics, he reached beneath his seat and recovered his ''shaving kit.'' Unzipping the case, he removed the semiautomatic it contained and slapped the clip in place. Jacking a round in the chamber, he tucked the gun in the back of his jeans. ''Your daughter…'' he said, returning the case to its hiding place. ''She's—''

''Just like me, sweetie.'' Babe smiled cheerfully, oblivious to what he'd been doing. ''I suggest you give in right here and now because you don't have a chance in the world of outmaneuvering that girl.''

He nodded. "That's what I thought."

She patted his arm. "It won't be so bad. Honest."

"I'll take your word for it." He scanned the hillside, looking for the best approach. "I don't suppose I can convince you to wait here?"

"I haven't changed my mind in the two minutes since we last discussed the possibility."

He wasn't surprised. Still, he'd been obligated to ask. "This is what I suggest. We'll take that path over there." He pointed. "And slip right up to the house. I'm hoping Reggie is as lax as your daughter about security and hasn't locked the back door."

"And then?"

"I'm going to open it and signal Loner." She wouldn't like this next part. "Loner will take Reggie down."

*"No!"*

"It's your daughter or your brother-in-law, Babe. Choose."

"There has to be another way." Tears burned her eyes, turning the blue incandescent. "I've lost enough people in my life. I can't stand to lose Reggie, too."

Oh, for— "Loner won't kill him," Noah explained gently. "He'll just…just gnaw on him a bit."

She rewarded his candor with a fist to his chest. "And I'm telling you Reggie wouldn't hurt Sami. If he's taken her, there's a good reason." She socked him again before he could avoid the blow. "I'm warning you, Hawke. If your mangy wolf does anything to hurt Reggie, I swear I'll never speak to you again. Do you hear me?"

"What about your daughter?" he practically roared.

"You find a way to get us in that cabin without any

injuries or I'll walk up to the front door and find out
what the hell is going on all by my lonesome. Do I make
myself perfectly clear?''

He didn't bother arguing. What was the point? ''We
don't even know if they're here. I suggest we take this
one step at a time.''

''I'll give you five minutes. Then I'm doing it my
way.''

''Fine.''

Grabbing her arm, he hustled her toward the path.
Trees and bushes helped conceal their approach. At the
edge of the tree line, Noah hesitated. Babe's guess had
been right, after all. The limo was parked at the side of
the house, though he couldn't see any movement coming
from the cabin.

''Keep down and take up a position on the left side
of the back door.'' She didn't reply, but the expression
in her eyes said it all. He sighed. ''I've changed the plan.
Loner won't hurt Reggie unless Sami's in imminent danger. I promise.''

''I expect you to keep that promise.'' Her breath shuddered from her lungs. ''Please.''

He would. He always did. ''Wait until I signal you,
then follow. Got it?''

Running in a crouch, Noah reached the back of the
cabin without arousing any attention. Hunkered down
against the wall, he gestured for Babe to follow. Once
they were in position, Loner slipped silently up to him
and crouched in preparation. This wasn't the first attack
drill they'd run. Reaching up, Noah softy turned the
doorknob, just enough to release the catch. It gave be-

neath his hand and he signaled Loner, repeating the gesture a second time to be certain the animal understood.

The instant he released the dog, Loner burst through the door with the sort of frenzied howl guaranteed to terrorize the most hearty souls. It ended abruptly, raising the hairs on the back of Noah's neck. Babe burst into tears, but he didn't have time to deal with her. Taking a deep breath, he burst through the door low, yanking his revolver free and training it on—

Uh-oh.

Sami and Reggie sat at a table, a hot-and-heavy gin rummy match going on between them. Instead of growling or howling or gnawing, Loner had plopped down between them, moaning in sheer delight as Sami scratched one ear and Reggie worked on the other. As far as Noah could tell, the only person in imminent danger was him.

Noah cleared his throat. "Reggie," he said with a nod. "Good to see you."

"And you, my boy." He lifted an eyebrow, eyeing the gun. "If you wanted to be dealt in, all you had to do was ask."

Sami slammed her cards to the table. "No, Uncle Reg," she bit out. "The line is… Is that a gun or are you just happy to see me?"

Reggie shrugged, sorting his cards. "I believe that expression works better for you than it would for me."

Sami fixed Noah with an infuriated glare. "Let me guess. That's the odd-shaped electric shaver you were in such a big hurry to hide in your drawer. Am I close?"

"Something like that." Releasing the clip from his gun, Noah ejected the round still in the chamber.

Reloading the bullet into the clip, he slipped it into his back pocket and tucked the gun out of sight in the waistband of his jeans. "I get the feeling I should give up shaving from now on."

Sami's eyes narrowed. "Wise decision."

"Reggie!" Babe came crashing through the back door just then. "Reggie, are you all right?"

"He wasn't the one abducted, Mom. I was," Sami thought to mention.

Noah's hands collapsed into fists. "Would someone please tell me what the *hell* is going on? Babe shows me blackmail notes addressed to Sami. Widget says Bill's abducted her. And I'm left holding a...a loaded shaver. Somebody better start explaining and fast."

"Reggie," Sami prompted gently. "It's time for the truth."

He lay down his cards with meticulous care. "Gin," he said.

"I'm serious."

"I know you are." His gaze didn't shift from the cards in front of him. "You also know I can't do that."

"Why don't I do it for you?"

"No, thank you, my dear." Very slowly he stood, adjusting his bow tie. "If everyone will excuse me, it's time I returned to the city."

Babe hastened to his side, grabbing his arm. "No. You aren't going anywhere until I get some answers."

Reggie carefully disengaged his arm from her grasp and stepped away. "Don't you understand, sweetheart? You're the one I can't tell." With that, he turned, his spine ruler-straight, and left the cabin.

"What have I done?" Babe whispered as the door

closed behind Reggie. "What have I done to lose his trust?"

Sami crossed to her mother's side. "You haven't done anything. He doesn't want to tell you the truth."

"What truth?" she demanded.

"He's broke, Mom."

"Broke?" She spun around. "No. That's not possible. The advertising business—"

"He sold it when Daddy died."

"But…*why?*"

"From what he's said—which isn't much—I gather that Dad was the idea man while Uncle Reggie took care of the details. Having seen him work with Widget and the other women, I'd say he excelled at his job. Unfortunately, without the ideas, the details didn't matter."

Babe stared in bewilderment. "But the business was worth a fortune. When he sold out, he should have been set for life."

Sami caught hold of her mother's hand. "Not if he gave it all away."

"Gave it away. Who would he…?" Her eyes widened in disbelief. "Oh, no. Oh, please, no."

"Dad bought the apartment and the house shortly before he died. Pacific Heights. Nob Hill. That's prime real estate. He used his share of the business as collateral. Uncle Reggie couldn't bear to see us turned out of our home. He made sure it didn't happen the only way he knew how."

"He didn't take anything?" Her voice broke. "Not a dime?"

"I think he believed he could start over, build a new fortune."

"And when he couldn't, he abducted you to recoup some of the money?" Babe shook her head. "No. I don't believe it. All he had to do was ask. I'd have given him whatever he needed."

"I suspect he'd have refused you," Noah interrupted. "He's a proud man."

Anger flared. "But it's okay to abduct my daughter?"

"That's not what happened." Sami wrapped an arm around her mother's shoulders. "I found out about his money problem years ago quite by accident. There was a mix-up at the bank. One of his business deals had gone sour and they called me, thinking I was his daughter. After that, I had a long talk with Bill and learned that every time Reggie lands on his feet, an old friend or a new friend or even a total stranger approaches looking for a handout."

Tears glittered in Babe's eyes. "He always was a sucker for a hard-luck story," she chided unevenly.

"You've been helping him, haven't you?" Noah asked Sami.

"He wouldn't take any money at first," she explained. "So I circumvented Reggie and told Bill to leave me a note whenever their finances were getting tight. Bill has a rather peculiar sense of humor and would leave these blackmail notes on the hallway table where I'd eventually find them. Whenever one arrived, I'd deposit funds directly into Reggie's account. But this time, something went wrong. I never received the message. I'd told Bill in the past that if our wires ever crossed, he was under strict orders to snatch me off the street, if necessary, but to make sure I got to the bank and took care of the problem.''

Noah made the connection from there. ''Got it. That's why Bill said he was following instructions.''

''Widget heard that, did she?'' Sami shrugged. ''After I transferred the funds over, I came up here to spend some time with Reggie. He'd been trying to talk to me for ages. He has some fantastic ideas for expanding my work project. Bill's intervention gave us the perfect opportunity to discuss them.'' Sami glanced from Noah to Babe. ''So what happened to the notes Bill left?''

Babe clasped her hands together. ''I found one right after I moved out. It was in with my mail.''

''As soon as she read it, she called me,'' Noah added. ''I have some experience helping people. I guess you could say I've made a career of it.''

Sami's narrowed gaze switched from him to her mother and back again. ''*That's* how you came to be my birthday present?''

Damn. Noah waited for the other shoe to drop. It didn't take long.

Anger flashed across her face, hot and furious. ''You're not really a man Friday, are you?''

''No.''

''Then what are you? Who are you?''

''I guess you could call me a troubleshooter. Basically I freelance aiding people who've gotten themselves into difficult predicaments and need assistance getting back out.'' He glanced at Babe. ''Mel pretty much determined my career path when I found myself cleaning up after him more times than I could count.''

"What did my mother ask you to do?" Sami asked. "Protect me?"

He inclined his head. "One secret bodyguard, at your service."

There was only one more question to ask and she didn't waste any time hitting him with it. "You never had any intention of getting me pregnant, did you? That was just an excuse to distract me until you could find the blackmailer."

"Pregnant?" Babe repeated. *"Pregnant?"*

His anger flared to match hers. "No, I never had any intention of getting you pregnant. And yes, I used it as an excuse to distract you until I could find the black-mailer." He stalked toward her, his gaze never leaving hers. "But just so you know, just so you're perfectly clear on this issue… I'd have said anything, done whatever it took, crossed every and all ethical lines I held dear to stop you from going through with that idiotic plan."

Her cropped shirt flickered in agitation, cavorting against her midriff. "Even sleep with me?"

He bared his teeth. "Hell, honey. I'd have even married you."

"That's it!" Sami spun on her bare heel—now why didn't that surprise him?—and stalked to the door. "I'm going home with Uncle Reggie."

Noah winced as the door slammed behind her. A painful silence descended and he shot Babe a wry look. "That went well, don't you think?"

Loner collapsed on the floor with a mournful whine.

Babe released her breath in a long sigh. "You know something, sweetie? I've been proposed to more times

than I can count. And I can categorically state with absolute and complete authority that that was the worst
proposal it's ever been my misfortune to hear.''

"Thanks.''

"Anytime.''


Noah walked into Sami Fontaine's residence and straight
into sheer chaos.

Men of every size, shape and description were scattered throughout the foyer. Some were seated in a row
of chairs lining the entranceway, others lounged on the
wide sweeping stairway leading to the second story. And
a few were even sprawled on the heartwood flooring.

"Something about this scene looks strangely familiar,'' Noah muttered. Glancing down at Loner, he gave
a quick signal. "You know what to do, boy. Get busy.''

He didn't wait to witness the results. Crossing the
foyer to the parlor door, he shoved it open. Sami sat
curled in a chair, her head entirely too close to the man
she was busy interviewing. Noah didn't waste any time.
In three easy strides, he had the no-longer-prospective
baby-maker out of the chair and drop-kicked from the
room. Slamming the door closed, he turned to face his
wife-to-be.

"Nice to see you again, too,'' she said tartly.

"Don't butter me up, sweetheart. I'm not in the
mood.''

She shot to her feet. "What are you so angry about?
I'm the one who should be furious. You and my mother
deceived me. If you'd bothered to ask me about those
notes, I could have straightened everything out in one

easy conversation. Instead you came charging in and I—''

To Noah's concern, her voice broke. ''Honey?''

When he would have approached, she waved him off, stalking out of reach. ''And I fell in love with you, you sorry excuse for a man Friday.'' She scowled at him over her shoulder. ''Now what are you doing here?''

''I came by to drop off my test results.'' He offered the paper with a flourish. ''You'll be pleased to know that I passed with flying colors and you won't need any baby-makers other than the one standing right in front of you. Mr. Perfect. Remember?''

''I'm thrilled. Put it on the desk and leave.''

He crumpled up the report and shot it with unerring accuracy into the trash basket beside the desk. ''I'm not going anywhere. Not until we've had time to discuss this.''

''There's nothing to discuss. You lied to me and I'm furious.''

''Funny. I could have sworn I heard you say that you loved me.''

''That, too.'' Her chin quivered. ''Why did you do it, Noah? Why didn't you explain everything when you first arrived?''

''Because I promised Babe I wouldn't.''

''You lied to me so you could keep your promise to her?''

''Something like that.'' He reached out and gently swept a tear from her cheek. ''I owed her, Sami. Or at least, I thought I did.''

''Why? Why did you owe her?''

It was time to tell her the truth. The whole truth. "It was an agreement we made."

"What sort of agreement?"

"She did me a favor. In exchange I promised to help out if she ever found herself in a jam."

He'd snagged her curiosity. "What was the favor?"

"She broke her engagement to my father. At my request."

It didn't take long for that to sink in. "Mel Hawke was your *father?*"

"*Is.* He is my father."

"And you…" She moistened her lips in a way that threatened to unman him. "You didn't want Mom to marry him?"

"I like Babe. She deserved better than dear old Dad. Still does, as far as I'm concerned." He shrugged. "I offered your mother anything she cared to name if she'd dump Mel. She agreed."

"I remember the stories you told about your father. You didn't owe her any favors. She owed you."

"It doesn't matter, Sami. She broke it off and that's all I cared about."

"Right up until she called the debt due." She wrapped her arms around her waist. "You must have been thrilled with the job she stuck you with."

"If you think I regret a single minute of it, think again." He approached. "You were the one stuck with the raw end of the deal. I'm sorry, honey. I should have been honest with you. If it helps, I promise it won't happen in the future."

"Why are you here, Noah?"

"You know why. I love you. And you love me, too. The only question is what we're going to do about it."

"Nothing is a distinct possibility."

"No, it's not. That's never been an option for us."

"Why did you have to lie to me, Noah? And I don't mean about Babe." Pain was implicit in every word. "Why did you have to offer yourself up as a father for my baby when you had no intention of going through with it?"

"Because I couldn't stand the idea of another man giving you what should only be created between the two of us."

Her mouth trembled and she pushed curls from her eyes, her bracelets clattering in agitation. "Are you offering for real this time?"

"If that's what you want."

She shook her head. "It's not."

Her whispered response hit like a blow. It took every bit of control he possessed to ask one final a question. "Why?"

"Because then you'll think having a baby is my main reason for marrying you."

The tightness in his chest eased ever so slightly. "And it's not?"

She shook her head. "If I were given the choice between you and a baby, I'd choose you."

"Even if it meant never having a child?"

"Yes."

She closed the distance between them. Barefoot and determined, she stood before him, a dynamic package of unstinting love. She expressed it in every movement, every breath and sound and look. It was in the wayward curls and the hopeful green eyes, the tremulous smile and musical clatter of her bracelets.

"I love you, Noah Hawke." She slipped her arms around his neck and waited. Releasing an impatient sigh, she prompted, "Now in case you didn't know the proper procedure here, you're supposed to say, 'I love you, too, Sami Fontaine.'"

"Not quite yet. Your mother told me I gave you the worst marriage proposal of any she's ever heard."

"Not to brag, but I suspect my mother could be considered an expert on the subject."

"Since I'm not planning on proposing marriage ever again, let me see if I can improve over last time."

A smile trembled free. "Give it your best shot."

He slipped his hands into sunshine, her curls wrapping around his fingers. And then he slanted his mouth over pure rapture. He took his time, easing the hurt with passionate understanding, proving in the only way he knew how that they were destined to share a rare and special love. She was so precious to him, a woman who held his life in her tender hands. He'd been a lone wolf long enough. He was mated to this woman, as surely as though she'd been imprinted on his soul. And he intended to stay by her side for the rest of their days. He waited until the comforting balm of his kiss had eased her distress, before pulling back.

"I'm sorry I hurt you, sweetheart. A man shouldn't hurt the woman he loves. And I do love you, Sami." He could have let it go at that. But she deserved more. Far more. "I've always known that someday I'd find the woman I'd spend the rest of my life with. You're my joy. My future. My life. And one day soon, I hope you'll be the mother of my children. You're everything I've ever wanted and everything I ever will need. Marry me, Sami.''

Tears filled her eyes. "No one, not even Babe, has had such a perfect proposal. Yes, I'll marry you.''

"No more fears?''

"None. Not anymore.''

He nodded in satisfaction. "Fair warning. I won't be satisfied until you have every one of those six children you've always wanted.''

Her smile turned impish. "Promise?''

"I always keep my promises.'' He hesitated. "I also have a confession to make.''

She sighed. "Another one?''

"I had Loner get rid of the baby-makers in the hall-way.''

"Er… Noah?''

"What is it, honey?''

"Those weren't potential baby-makers. Remember my conversation with Reggie? Working with Widget has been such a success, I've decided to expand my job placement project. Those were people I was interviewing for the position.''

"I have a suggestion. Forget them and hire Reggie. A successful business can always use a good detail man. Besides, I think he'll feel better receiving a salary than charity, don't you?''

"Not that he'll need it.''

Noah lifted an eyebrow. "You don't think so?''

She grinned. "Not if Babe has her way. I suspect Mother's sixth and last marriage is in the offing.''

Catching Noah's hand in hers, she started toward the door. "Come on, buster. We have work to do."

"Work?" Damn. "Don't you want to celebrate our engagement first?"

"I sure do. I thought we'd celebrate by practicing."

"Practicing?"

She glanced over her shoulder, filling his life with the joy of her laughter. "If we're going to have six kids, we can use all the practice we can get, don't you think?"

He swept her into his arms and carried her into the foyer. "Honey, forget about thinking. I suggest we get right to the doing."

In the distance he heard Loner howl, a long, oddly happy sound. And then, to his astonishment the call was answered.

"That reminds me," Sami said, linking her fingers at the base of his neck. "We have new neighbors. And they have the oddest-looking dog. If I didn't know better, I'd swear it was a wolf. A female, if I'm not mistaken."

Noah sighed. "By the sound of things, we might have to change Loner's name."

"I suspect you're right." She dropped her head to his shoulder. "How does Mr. and Mrs. Woof grab you?"

**MILLS & BOON®**

*Makes*
*any time*
*special*

Enjoy a romantic novel from
*Mills & Boon*®

*Presents...*™  *Enchanted*™  TEMPTATION®

*Historical Romance*™  ⊬**MEDICAL ROMANCE**™

MAT1

# MILLS & BOON®

## Enchanted™

### THE SHEIKH'S REWARD by Lucy Gordon

Frances wanted an interview with Sheikh Ali Ben Saleem, and he agreed—on condition she accompany him to his kingdom. Once there, however, Frances found herself imprisoned by his concubines! What was more...Ali was insisting on marriage...

### BRIDE ON LOAN by Leigh Michaels

Caleb Tanner needs a decoy to save him from the many women scheming to get him to the altar! Sabrina isn't thrilled about moving in with Caleb. He's too attractive for his own good. He's also her agency's biggest client so she has no choice but to play the bride-to-be.

### HONEYMOON HITCH by Renee Roszel

Jake has made it clear that he wants children from his marriage of convenience with Susan. Yet, while Susan yearns for Jake's love without having even experienced a kiss from him, the most daunting thing on the horizon isn't their wedding day...but their wedding night!

### A WIFE AT KIMBARA by Margaret Way

Brod Kinross suspects Rebecca of being a gold-digger, after his father's money. In fact it's not the money that Rebecca wants—or Brod's father—it's love and marriage to Brod himself...

## *Available from 5th May 2000*

*Available at most branches of WH Smith, Tesco, Martins, Borders, Easons, Volume One/James Thin and most good paperback bookshops*

0004/02

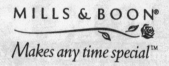

# 2 FREE

## books and a surprise gift!

We would like to take this opportunity to thank you for reading this Mills & Boon® book by offering you the chance to take TWO more specially selected titles from the Enchanted™ series absolutely FREE! We're also making this offer to introduce you to the benefits of the Reader Service™—

> ★ FREE home delivery
> ★ FREE gifts and competitions
> ★ FREE monthly Newsletter
> ★ Exclusive Reader Service discounts
> ★ Books available before they're in the shops

Accepting these FREE books and gift places you under no obligation to buy, you may cancel at any time, even after receiving your free shipment. Simply complete your details below and return the entire page to the address below. *You don't even need a stamp!*

**YES!** Please send me 2 free Enchanted books and a surprise gift. I understand that unless you hear from me, I will receive 4 superb new titles every month for just £2.40 each, postage and packing free. I am under no obligation to purchase any books and may cancel my subscription at any time. The free books and gift will be mine to keep in any case.

N0EA

Ms/Mrs/Miss/Mr ..............................Initials................................
BLOCK CAPITALS PLEASE

Surname ......................................................................................

Address ......................................................................................

........................................................................................................

..............................................Postcode..................................

**Send this whole page to:**
**UK: FREEPOST CN81, Croydon, CR9 3WZ**
**EIRE: PO Box 4546, Kilcock, County Kildare (stamp required)**

Offer valid in UK and Eire only and not available to current Reader Service subscribers to this series. We reserve the right to refuse an application and applicants must be aged 18 years or over. Only one application per household. Terms and prices subject to change without notice. Offer expires 31st October 2000. As a result of this application, you may receive further offers from Harlequin Mills & Boon and other carefully selected companies. If you would prefer not to share in this opportunity please write to The Data Manager at the address above.

Mills & Boon® is a registered trademark owned by Harlequin Mills & Boon Limited. Enchanted™ is being used as a trademark.